BOUND IN GLORY

KEN HUDSON

BOUND IN
GLORY

KEN HUDSON

Thank you for buying this book's authorized edition and complying with copyright laws. For wholesale inquiries, please reach out to this email address: boundinglory.hudson@gmail.com

Published by Radiant Publishing
Paperback ISBN: 978-1-963922-14-1
Hardback ISBN: 978-1-963922-15-8
Ebook ISBN: 978-1-963922-13-4

First Edition | Printed in the United States

Contents

CHAPTER ONE

Quake

Rayford Witt started his day like any other with a shower in his room at the Saint Regis Hotel in Cairo, Egypt. The small soap always seemed to slip out of his big hands, but he was used to it by now. He couldn't help but think about the convenience of liquid soap back in America. Ray's 6'2" frame always seemed too large for standard hotel accommodations; his elbows hit the walls and shower curtain while he washed up. But that's just who Ray was, a man's man.

It was just another day on duty in a foreign country. Ray was in Egypt to cover a story about the current Prime Minister, Mostafa Al-Katib, a former Egyptian army officer turned politician. Capital Cable Journal News (CCJN), who Ray worked for, had finagled a personal interview with this complicated politician and family man. As a journalist, Ray was a little nervous about his first on-camera work. He had spent the past fifteen years with the company behind the camera producing and writing, but now the focus would be on him. Opening the wall closet to the neatly pressed and stylish clothes awaiting him, he carefully selected a suit that fit his business-like conservative style, which others expected of him even outside of work. He knew he fit the tall, dark, and handsome stereotype, and he embraced it.

A quick glance at the clock confirmed he was right on schedule. Ray despised being late and hated when others were late too. As he buttoned up his crisp white shirt, he glanced at himself in the mirror, adjusting his tie, perfectly centering it. As he put on one sock, then one shoe, followed by the other sock and shoe, Ray chuckled at the thought of having to hop out of the hotel sock- or shoeless if there were ever a fire.

As he bent over to put on his second shoe, he nearly fell on the floor. *Hmm, that's odd,* he thought. Ray didn't drink and he certainly didn't have a hangover. *Maybe my balance is just off. No, that's not it.* The entire room moved from side to side and tossed him to the floor, like a roller coaster with the room as the coaster car, no seat belt to hold him in place.

He quickly scrambled toward the nearest door frame, heart pounding in his chest. The deafening roar of the earthquake drowned out any other sound, and the air filled up thick with dust. As he clung to the frame, his mind raced with thoughts of survival. He had faced danger countless times in his adventurous life. At forty-two, Ray had experienced much—the slaughter of monks in the highland mountains of Tibet to living with the four-foot indigenous natives of South America. But this was somehow different—nature's wrath unleashed. In the chaos, his instincts kicked in. He had to find a way out before the shaking intensified or the building collapsed entirely.

Most seasoned travelers know better than to stay on the forty-second floor of a hotel. After all, a fire truck's ladder cannot reach that high. In a fire, he'd be doomed. *Why did I ask for the top floor?* It made no sense now. He was stuck in this tower during a 9.0 earthquake. *Do I have a death wish? Maybe I want to just die and be free,* for freedom had eluded him his entire life. His heart sank as cracks spiderwebbed across the concrete structure, a clear sign of imminent danger. The deafening sound of crashing furniture and shattering glass echoed through the air, drowning out his thoughts.

Ray wondered if this was the big one he had read about in Scripture: *"For nation shall rise up against nation, and kingdom against kingdom; and there shall be famine, and pestilences, and earthquakes, in diverse places."*[1]

Is the building really collapsing? He watched as cement crumbled and dust clouded the air, obscuring his view of the sky above. It was an odd perspective, seeing the sky from above rather than through a window.

Ray was known as pragmatic and dependable, but this situation challenged his status quo. How would he explain himself after this disaster? The luxurious five-star hotel crumpled before his eyes, each floor toppling onto the next like a game of dominoes. As he watched expensive fixtures from the penthouse fall, their once-important details seemed completely insignificant in the face of this destruction.

The rugs remained tightly fixed to the falling floors, their intricate Persian designs depicting dragons and samurai stuck in a state of chaos. They coexisted with cheap throw rugs, likely purchased from a nearby market near the Hyatt Cairo. Shattered glass littered the ground; its sharp shards threatening to pierce skin and stick there. Large chunks of debris fell according to the physics of size, weight, and girth. Amongst it all lay mangled pieces of iron, steel rods, aluminum, and other metals.

The maid's cart, previously stocked with neatly folded toiletries, bars of soap, and cheap little lotions had flung its contents in a chaotic frenzy. Ray felt the

---

[1] Matthew 24:7 NKJV

strangeness of considering such mundane things while faced with impending doom—screams surrounded him as people met their own tragic fates.

Ray observed the sheer terror and panic that this seismic event ignited. He had seen the look of death before on those already gone and those who knew they would soon meet their end. But the sounds truly haunted him—the deafening noise of the massive structure crumbling to the ground, followed by the distinct cries of pain as people were crushed beneath beds of concrete and steel. Despite his own fear, his thoughts turned toward those suffering and perishing around him.

Having witnessed wars, accidents, and even some murders in the past, he couldn't help but think of them now. But in reality, it didn't matter how many times he saw death—the feeling never changed. It was a stark reminder of his humanity, no matter what tragedies he had seen or experienced. He couldn't kid himself; he never got used to it. His heart, his humanity, his Savior wouldn't let him forget . . . We are all just flesh and blood.

He plummeted down, his body colliding with a hard chunk of cement. He knew immediately his third rib fractured on impact, causing sharp pain in his chest that made it difficult to breathe. He tasted the metallic tang of blood in his throat because of his punctured lung, it trickled out of his nose as he gasped for air. Once again, he was fading away from life. Back home, his wife Monica had no idea.

Suburban life in Pelham, a small borough on the north side of New York City, was always pleasant during this time of year. Birds actively built their nests and prepared for the hatchlings soon to come. Nature awakened to the new spring season with petunias, marigolds, and asters dotting the landscape. Every form of new life had birthed right outside Monica and Ray's modern condominium.

The alarm went off and Monica's long, sleek arm fumbled for the sleep button, of course knocking the buzzing nuisance to the floor. She groaned as she swung her legs over the side of the bed and stretched her arms above her head. The early morning sunlight streamed through the curtains, casting a warm glow across the room. She took a moment to appreciate the life she and Ray had created together. Running a hand through her tousled hair, she sighed and whispered, "Thank you, Lord. We are truly blessed!"

The warm water of the shower cascaded down her petite body and revitalized her. Monica's hair was undeniably beautiful, and many people admired it as her most attractive feature. As for Ray, it was love from the first moment he saw her, proving that love at first sight still exists in a world of impulsivity and lustful desires.

As the light shone upon her beautiful brown skin, she couldn't help but notice the minor faults in her manicure. The polish on a few of her nails had chipped, disrupting her otherwise put-together appearance. She followed a simple rule: Hands and feet couldn't be neglected. No matter how stylish an outfit may be, if these details weren't maintained, you were just wasting your time. In her mind, people might not comment on them directly, but they definitely noticed. And for someone respectable like Monica, this was simply not cool.

But she wasn't expecting any guests. Yesterday, she had spent a lovely day out with friends shopping and chatting, but today she returned to her post-COVID in-home routine, back in her cozy pajamas. She turned on her computer as she fixed her morning coffee. Mrs. Rayford Witt had specific requirements for this—the coffee must be freshly ground and used the same day; she always bought just enough for the week. As Monica precisely ground the beans and prepared her cup of Joe, she turned on her favorite smooth jazz station on the stereo.

Memories flooded back of the concert she and Ray had attended two weeks ago, listening to the smooth sounds of saxophonist Marcus Benjamin. They discovered their shared love for jazz in their early days of dating. As Monica listened to the mellow tones of the bass and drums filling their condo, she couldn't help but feel a sense of longing for Ray while he was away on assignment. *Why do I feel kinda blue today?* she wondered. *Today isn't different than any other day when he's gone.*

With the first sip, she could always tell if she had achieved the perfect ratio of water to beans in her coffee. After adding just the right amount of creamer, she took a moment to appreciate her mastery of this daily ritual with a chuckle. She leaned back in her executive chair and opened her computer, noting five unread messages waiting for her attention. *I guess my clients are eager to start the day! It'd really be wise to finish what I've already started before getting sidetracked with a new task,* but her curiosity got the best of her. She clicked on the first message in her work email. It caught her attention:

Dear Ms. Witt,

My name is Justin O'Neil, and I have a request for you. As someone who has been raised in foster homes my entire life, I am determined to uncover information about my biological family and learn more about my own identity. If you could assist me in this search, it would mean a great deal to me.

Could we please schedule a call at your convenience? You can reach me at 590-877-9645 to discuss the details.

Sincerely,
Justin O'Neil

Monica felt deeply for Justin's situation, but this wasn't the type of work she was used to. She was a skilled genealogist with a college degree, and her job revolved around uncovering family history—for a price, of course. She specialized in tracing bloodlines back hundreds of years, not aiding orphaned children. Monica took pride in her work, and she excelled at her job.

Dear Justin,

I am a genealogist, and although I have expertise in tracing family histories, finding lost parents is not within my area of knowledge. It may be beneficial for you to hire a private investigator or utilize one of the family lineage websites. I regret that I cannot assist you, but I wish you the best of luck.

Best regards,
Monica Witt

She then went on to message two.

> To Whom It May Concern,
>
> I am writing to request your assistance with tracing my family history for our upcoming family reunion next year. My name is Matthew Chambers, and I am the committee chair for this event. We have allocated a budget to ensure the accuracy of the information we receive. If you are interested in taking on this project, please contact me at 555-284-4002. I am located in Buffalo, New York, so please keep in mind the Eastern Time Zone when calling (as I tend to go to bed early).
>
> Sincerely,
> Matt Chambers

The sultry music playing in the background seemed to match Monica's mood as she swayed along with its rhythm. Her foot tapped on the floor as she thought about how her bank account would remain steady thanks to this successful career. She allowed herself to relax for a moment before moving on to the task at hand.

Satisfaction filled Monica as she put the final touches on her current assignment. This job had been a huge undertaking, demanding much in both effort and time. She had already received the promised $15,000 down payment for the investigation—digging into the background of the founder of a liberal arts college—and now, two months later, it was time to collect the remaining $10,000. Jobs like this didn't come around often. In addition to traversing her hometown in upscale Philly, the assignment had required travel to Virginia, the Carolinas, and eventually Maryland.

On to message three:

> Have you got debt? We can help you escape this obligation and
> put you on the road to prosperity! How? By . . .

DELETE!

As Monica finished reading through her messages, a news report on the radio suddenly interrupted her life. "A 9.0 magnitude earthquake has just struck Cairo, Egypt today, and there are reports of thousands dead or missing." Her heart sank and she dropped to her knees, lightheaded, as if she were about to faint. She had the same sinking feeling of losing her wallet, magnified a hundred times over. Shock and panic, like when you see your own blood pouring from a deep cut. How is it in moments like this, you just know that someone you love is in danger? Is it some kind of supernatural bond beyond the physical? How is it that life can turn you upside down in an instant? The feeling is inexplicable, but somehow, you just know.

On her knees, Monica was naturally inclined to cry out to the Lord. "Please God, keep Ray safe!" But deep down, she knew he wasn't. Her tears flowed freely, and her stomach churned with worry. In this desperate moment, the truth of 1 Corinthians 10:13 came flooding into her mind: God will never allow you to be tempted beyond what you can bear. She had heard it countless times since her youth in Sunday School. As she looked up at the sky for guidance, she sought refuge in the words of Psalm 121: *I lift up my eyes to the mountains—where does my help come from? My help comes from the Lord, the Maker of heaven and earth.*[2] They brought comfort to her soul, reaching places that only God could touch.

Monica had a close relationship with Christ and had accepted Him as her personal Savior many years ago. She had met Ray at God's New Covenant Church five years prior during a singles' dinner, and she still faithfully attended services there on Sundays and a women's Bible study group on Tuesdays. But this disaster truly tested her faith, for the first time. *Could I handle never seeing Ray again? Could I cope if his body were never found, buried under the rubble, or destroyed in an explosion of debris and wires?*

How do all the praise and worship songs I've sung, all my tithes, all the Spirit-filled sermons I'ved listened to, apply right now, in real time? I'm landing on the worst-case scenario without having all the facts, she reminded herself. Her murmurings to God became audible. *God, be my "very present help" in trouble.*

Suddenly, she heard God's still, small voice urging her, *Trust in My plan for your life.*

Moment by moment, she prayed for guidance. *God, give me the power and strength to make this call.* As she moved from two knees to one foot up, she continued, *God, I will trust your Word.* She stood to make her way to the ringing phone and determined, *Not my will, but Yours be done.* As she picked up the phone she cleared her voice. "Hello?"

---

[2] Verses 1–2 NIV

CHAPTER TWO

Attitudes

Tanya had worked halfway through her garbage collection route as her truck rolled up to the apartment complex, its loud engine and thick exhaust fumes impossible to miss, and a common sight in the neighborhood as it came and went on its appointed days. *Couldn't the city invest in quieter, more environmentally friendly garbage trucks?* she half-wondered, half-complained.

Tanya simply wanted to make good money as part of New York City's sanitation crew, and her tough attitude had won her the title "sanitation queen" in her district. It would soon be her turn to take the wheel, and she couldn't wait. Her arms felt tired from yesterday's exhausting trash run, where every bin seemed to overflow—just another one of those hard days all blue-collar workers dread, when Monday feels like it's dragging on forever and Friday can't come soon enough. These apartments signified the halfway point of the day—not just a lunch break but a hump break.

RJ, her partner, yelled to the back of the truck. "Gimme some guidance! I can't see anything out the right side." No response. He shouted louder, frustrated. "Tanya! What's goin' on back there? Can't you hear me?" With screeching brakes and a slamming door, RJ's aggression showed itself. Old habits die hard and some things never change, especially for a West Side ex-gang member. *She's not the only one with an attitude!* he thought.

Since she was nowhere in sight of his mirrors he hopped out of the truck to search for her. RJ had learned to control his anger, depending on who he was dealing with. At the drop of a hat, he could switch from intimidating to gentle as a warm southern breeze. Everyone knew about his past, about the time he spent in juvie, but they had grace; after all, everyone has a past.

Tanya was sitting on the concrete just behind the truck near an opened box. She had scattered magazines and books from it across the ground near a garbage bin, then neatly laid her gloves on top of the scattered debris. She was reading a book with unusual care and interest, an unexpected sight for a garbage collector. The book had completely engrossed her, much like a child discovering *Where the Wild Things Are* for the first time. RJ couldn't help but pause a moment as he approached, surprised by her tenderness as she delicately turned each page.

Collecting himself, he let out a booming yell down the alleyway, like a quarterback calling out plays. "What the hell were you thinking, girl?! You could have gotten yourself killed!" His words echoed off the graffiti-covered walls, causing an instinctive reaction in a few souls around the nearby projects. Some ran to their windows to see the struggle; other onlookers froze in place, wondering why the usual Wednesday sounds of trucks and screeching brakes were interrupted by an angry Black man's shouts at 9:10 a.m.

Tanya's demeanor shifted as the enchantment of the box faded, revealing her notorious attitude. She tossed the book carelessly back into the box and marched toward RJ, signaling a looming confrontation. Her mind raced, preparing for battle.

"Alright, let's go!" someone called out from a nearby window. Then, "Hey Maxine, you gotta see this!"

Tanya's voice boomed back at RJ. "Who are you yellin' at?" She put her gloves back on and prepared herself for action, her 120-pound frame ready for any challenge. "RJ, you know I don't play those games. You better get it right and show some respect." Growing up on the tough streets had taught RJ common sense; this wasn't a battle worth fighting. He had been partners with Tanya about a year and was well aware of her explosive temper. Giving in was not an option for her and never would be.

Management had deliberately paired them together to meet the state's affirmative action requirements. They hired a woman and an African American to balance out a system still plagued by racism. The local managers expected the former gang member and fiery feminist activist to clash so one of them would eventually leave, but one year later, the duo proved them wrong.

RJ simply raised his hand and silently made his way back to his seat in the truck. Not another word.

At least two onlookers from the upper windows expressed their disappointment, firing out curses common and even expected in the environment. But soon enough, things settled back into the usual routine of the ghetto, surroundings that had become all too familiar to them both.

CHAPTER THREE

Devastating News

Approximately seven hours earlier, Monica had first heard about the earthquake in Egypt on the radio. Feeling numb and aimless, she paced around her condo, hoping for any news or updates about the situation upending her life. Waiting was agony.

A ringtone suddenly sounded on her phone, one she recognized instantly. She picked up. "Hello Monica, it's Steve Moore. Have you heard about the situation in Egypt?" She tapped into the strength of her recent prayers and shoved out her nervousness, responding with a confident "Yes, I know about the earthquake, but not the details. What's happening there?"

"The epicenter of the earthquake was in Cairo." As program director for CCJN, Steve was known for speaking directly and being directive. Monica respected that, but she wasn't in the mood to hear a blunt and insensitive update about her husband.

"I see," she replied calmly, but struggled hard to maintain her composure. "Please continue."

"Currently, the information from Cairo is incomplete and unreliable. However, according to reports, the hotel where Ray and his team were staying was completely decimated by the quake. It leveled the entire building. Rescue teams from various countries are rushing to Egypt to aid in the aftermath of this tragedy. The U.S. has also offered help, and the Red Cross is on their way. The U.N. has sent peacekeeping forces. As for the downtown area surrounding the hotel, it is estimated at 90 percent destroyed with very few survivors. Helicopters and fire trucks are working tirelessly to extract individuals from the rubble; the hospitals are overwhelmed with patients."

"Steve," Monica interrupted, "this isn't a news report, it's my husband, okay?"

Steve continued as if he didn't even hear her. "We don't have any definite information about Ray's condition at this time. But based on the current situation, it does not look promising. It appears there may have been no survivors. I'm truly sorry, Monica."

Tears streamed down her cheeks, her heart aching at the thought of life without Ray. She struggled to hold back her emotions.

"I'm sorry," Steve said sincerely. "You know I loved Ray too."

Monica's questions tumbled out in desperate and hysterical tones. "Why are you talking like he's dead? Did something happen? Was there a body?"

A doorbell interrupted her breakdown. "Steve, someone's at the door, I'll call you back."

"Wait," Steve pleaded, "I know who it is . . . Wait!" Monica's emotions spilled over into sobs—grief, anxiety, emotional exhaustion—all rolled into one. He continued. "We arranged for transportation to pick you up and take you directly to the airport. From there, you and a few other employees from CCJN will board our private jet to Cairo."

Even in the midst of his brief lack of sensitivity, Steve and CCJN remained a top-notch company, evidenced by this kind gesture. "I'll be waiting at the airport to meet you, Monica. I'll also be joining you on the trip to Egypt."

"But I haven't packed. I'm not ready to go anywhere," Monica protested.

"Take your time. The driver will wait for you," Steve reassured her. "Are you alright, Monica?" Silence. Her numb, overwhelmed spirit failed to respond. She simply pressed the red button on her phone without a final word or farewell.

She made her way to the door and greeted the elderly driver from CCJN. "Please return in an hour or so; I'll gather my belongings," she requested.

"Of course, ma'am. My name is Horace, and I'll wait as long as you need me to," he replied kindly. "I'm a very patient man." Monica invited him inside to wait. "Thank you," he declined, "but I'll wait in the car out front. I have some reading to do while you get ready," he said with a smile. "The Good Book teaches us to wait on the Lord patiently, and I can wait for you too!"

"Are you reading the Bible?" Monica inquired. Horace nodded proudly. "Would you mind praying for me on our way to the airport?" she asked tentatively. "My husband is missing in Cairo. Without hesitation, Horace removed his hat and offered a prayer for strength, and for a miracle in Egypt. "Thank you, Mr. Horace," she said gratefully.

"I should go pack now," she said as she turned and left to gather her belongings. A unique sense of peace washed over her from the encounter.

Ray crashed onto the ground, surrounded by a chaotic mass of rubble and bodies in various stages of destruction. He lay among piles of twisted metal, broken concrete, and shattered bodies. The sounds of agony filled his ears as he lay still, deep inside the massive heap, once a beautiful, modern, state-of-the-art hotel that had turned into a tomb.

He surveyed his injuries. *This must be what people mean when they say, "I'll break every bone in your body."* Without question, that had nearly happened to him. Some bones protruded through his skin, like the jagged edge of his tibia. Others hid beneath swollen bruises and twisted lumps all over his body. Blood coated everything, some from him and some from others. The warm wound on his neck still oozed red and white—a fatal injury for anyone else.

He noticed a hole in his right arm and immediately moved to patch it up. But as he reached for it, something felt off, way off. The joint had partially separated, and his arm appeared like a tangle of red wires with veins and ligaments dangling from the open flesh. Luckily, Ray had always been ambidextrous and could use both hands equally well. He turned to assess the condition of his left hand. As he did so, a spurt of blood erupted from the wound on his neck. Surprisingly, the middle finger of his left hand managed to stop the bleeding, at least for a brief moment.

The thick smoke enveloping downtown Cairo, where luxurious hotels and beautiful buildings once stood, resembled a sandstorm straight from the depths of the Sahara Desert. This was not an uncommon sight in Egypt, as seasonal red winds from the south occasionally whipped up clouds of dust that smoothed out the faces of the majestic pharaohs and towering pyramids. The streets had filled with clouds of gas and debris, making it nearly impossible to see or breathe, reminiscent of the 9/11 devastation later revealed by satellite images.

The white asbestos monster raced through the streets of Egypt's largest city, engulfing everything in its path. People from all walks of life—Africans, Asians, Europeans, Americans, tourists, residents, hustlers, beggars, cabbies—fled for their lives as the sun disappeared behind a dense blanket of smoke.

Ray's body went limp as he felt the beam beneath him shift, causing him to slip down farther from the top of the pile and into a small gap between concrete slabs. Sudden darkness engulfed him as dust and debris previously clouding his sight vanished, leaving him trapped in a five-by-seven-foot prison.

A cool breeze drifted up from the wreckage below, and the sickening stench of death hit Ray's nose. He had spent a lot of time surrounded by death and decay, yet here it overcame him.

If his expensive watch were still working, it would have registered over thirty hours that he had been trapped under the collapsed building. The word *ruins* came to mind in this place of pharaohs and pyramids. The Nile River flowed through this land of ancient wonders, of tombs and caves that baffled scientists, who speculated that aliens built them. The powerful pharaohs and queens of this civilization were buried with extravagant riches, with gold, silver, and perfumes. Ray chuckled at the irony, at the absurdity, knowing he sat just a few miles from the majestic Pyramids of Giza, stuck in a mangled home of iron and cement. The African sun had long since set, leaving Ray's bed, a slab of cement, cold and sheathed in darkness.

The emptiness in his stomach echoed throughout the darkness, bouncing off the walls and into the abyss below. Boredom set in. Ray's injuries had completely healed, not a scratch remained, even though dried blood still caked his shirt. Death's failed attempt to claim his life troubled him. He let out an exasperated sigh as he took in the scene around him. He muttered, "Jesus, how on earth am I going to explain this one?"

The sounds of human activity and machinery above announced a rescue on its way. The blood on his clothes clearly displayed his formerly broken bones and injuries, yet visible wounds on his skin no longer existed. Others would surely question how it was possible.

The mice, rats, beetles—creatures that thrived on death—scurried around, feasting on waste, along with maggots left behind by flies. Death predators, you might say. They were surprisingly quick in their natural habitat, using speed, darkness, surprise, and stealth to their advantage. But the biggest problem by far was the rats. They ruled this place, constantly causing trouble for Ray. He barely had space enough to let them know he wasn't dead. Every day, without fail, one particularly pesky rat would appear, challenging Ray to an unending game of cat and mouse. Ray could only get rid of this particular varmint by killing it.

Surrounded by an abundance of food, Ray couldn't comprehend why "Spot" so fixated on tearing pieces of flesh from his body. The only logical explanation was the challenge and thrill of outsmarting Ray, live prey. This rodent wanted to assert his dominance over its trapped victim. But Ray refused to be a passive target in the game this mouse forced him to play. The rogue beast, with its shifty pink eyes and lightning-fast movements, would not stop attacking him.

In a twisted way, Ray found himself strangely exhilarated by the challenge. It provided a welcome break from the endless hours of monotony and dullness. He had no fear of permanent injury, as his previous bites had already healed; even the broken knuckles from trying to punch the perpetrator had returned to their original state. However, simply swinging or kicking at Spot in self-defense wasn't enough; Ray would have to take a more proactive approach in this battle.

Spot's go-to plan: attacking Ray from behind, targeting his head. Ray couldn't forget the rat's gross, coarse tail brushing against his neck during their last encounter; now he listened vigilantly, carefully, for any approaching sounds. He knew timing would be crucial; once he heard the scurrying of claws on the smooth cement, he would need to get ready. If not, it would mean another victory for Spot. He quickly assessed the space around him, mentally visualizing the dimensions to strategically position his head while keeping his arms free to move.

Ray had plenty of time. He spent hours meticulously, mentally measuring this tomb. He started with his fingertips, then moved on to his elbow and shoulder. With arms stretched wide, he measured from fingertip to fingertip. At a solid 6'2", he estimated the small cave to be about seven feet long and five feet wide, give or take a few inches. It would be difficult but essential to figure out all the openings a determined rat could squeeze through. He wasn't excited about running his hand along every wall, sticking it in every crevice, knowing the sharp incisors of his opponent awaited him, but he needed to tackle this challenge.

CHAPTER FOUR

Night Shift in Hangar 7

The noise of jet engines, a constant mix of loud roaring and high-pitched whining, grated on Antonio's nerves. He ached for his shift to end; the sweat stains on his shirt testified to the drudgery of a tough day on the job, one of those hot ones in Jersey when you feel like you're wading through a river of humidity. His cut biceps, accentuated by a rolled-up muscle shirt, revealed his great physical shape at age thirty-two. His tool cabinet, on the other hand, showed signs of wear and tear from years of use, but Tony knew exactly where to find every wrench and hammer he needed. Today's task? Breaking down a troublesome L-1011 Lockheed turbo engine to pinpoint why it wouldn't run at full capacity.

The majority of the process took place in his mind, since the engine was still attached to the plane's wing. The large cavity of the twin-turbo engine enabled a person to easily move around inside, and Tony's 5'10" frame fit comfortably. His expertise in troubleshooting had landed him a job with Wings over America Airlines and a hefty six-figure salary. As a skilled craftsman, he loved creating and fixing things with his hands.

"Freddie, can you bring the ladder over to the L-Bird engine?" Tony called out to his apprentice, an intern engine mechanic first-grade. "I need to check out the carbon-fiber blade panel."

"On it, Tony," Freddie quickly responded. "Can I come up and assist you, boss? I could use some practice with the L-panel blades."

"Not this time. I need you in the cockpit activating the controls for me. Don't forget your headset."

"Yes, sir. I've got it under control."

Tonys' mind wandered to Julie, who he had been married to for twelve years, a loving and passionate wife. They had been together a long time, but never chose to have children. In fact, Tony had made it a top priority to marry someone who felt at peace without kids. The pain of losing his only son in the past was too much to bear; he never wanted to experience it again. He found comfort in the idea of seeing his son in heaven someday, yet the memories of his loss never faded away. Some wounds run too deep for time alone to heal.

Julie was unable to bear children. She was a stunning woman; her thick, fiery red hair cascaded down her back like molten lava, adding to her already striking appearance. She had overcome anger issues in her youth, crediting a passing belief in God with carving out a more even-tempered character. Tony only knew this stable side of Julie, and felt he had found his perfect match in this beautiful woman. Even at thirty-five years, Mrs. Julie Amanda Hall looked youthful and radiant, just like her husband. They were an ideal couple, and by faith, Tony believed they would spend eternity together.

He gathered the tools he needed to replace the turbofan blade and panel reset and made his way to the engine ramp. He reached the foot of the ramp's stairs, then donned his headset and activated his communication system. Switching to channel 3, he called out, "Freddie, are you there? Testing—one, two, three." No response.

He grabbed the handrails for safety and proceeded up the steep fifteen-foot metal ramp slick with oil and moisture, toward the internal components of the RB211 engine, while intermittently repeating his test. He stepped into the engine and heard a click in his earpiece. A familiar voice came through. "Hello, hello, are you there, boss?" Freddie asked.

Tony adjusted the headset volume and sound burst into his left ear. He jumped, then quickly turned it down. "I can hear you, Fred," he replied with a hint of frustration. "Removing the turbofan panel now. Stand by to switch on overhead panel system three."

"Copy that, Tony," Freddie promptly responded.

Tony removed the panel, revealing a maze of wires and computer chips, enough to make heads spin. But Tony wasn't like most people; he was in a league of his own. Each exposed wire, chip, and capacitor received meticulous testing and inspection. His years of experience had trained him to focus on the most likely source of the problem, starting with simpler components and gradually moving to more complex ones. Typically, he could trace issues like this back to switch RZ6A, the brains of the unit that controlled the power flow through it.

He carefully removed the master chip and tested it; it seemed to function fine. To rule out any false readings, he double-checked the next chip in line, known to give inaccurate readings. Once satisfied, he activated his transmitter and radioed Fred. "Turn on overhead engine panel RZ6A for two or three seconds."

"Affirmative, sir," Freddie responded.

Tony heard the sweet hum of the electrical current as it shot through the circuit and registered *functioning properly*. The big fan on his left fired up and spun half a revolution in a three-second burst. *First two chips, check,* he noted mentally. He repeated this process for the next half hour, and each system checked out perfectly. The clock ticked closer to four o'clock.

Tony spoke again, authoritative and firm. "Fred, I'm running a comprehensive system check on module LCD2A, over." After a moment of silence, he tried again. "Fred, just to confirm, I am currently checking module LCD2A—that's L like Larry, C like Charlie, D like David, 2A. Can you confirm receipt?" No response from the cockpit. *Are my batteries dying? What's going on?* "Fred, can you confirm my previous transmission about the system check? Fred, can you hear me?" he asked urgently. "Run a complete system check, stat! Can you do that?"

"Roger that," Fred replied, but too late. The once pleasant hum of power running through the unit turned sour.

The massive spinning engine blade on Tonys' right fully engaged, and the worst-case scenario for an airplane mechanic sprang to life. In panic, Tony dropped his handheld unit and stumbled over his tools. "Critical Red! Critical Red!" he shouted, forgetting to hit SEND on his transmitter. Once he realized this, it was too late. His body fell onto the smooth metal engine hub, hands frantically grasping for something to hold on to. Only a few moments remained before the metal mass of the engine would completely swallow him.

CHAPTER FIVE

Departures

Though he was alive and in good health, Ray despised his confinement in this small, timeless space. Day and night held no distinction. At least the constant drone of machinery above him provided some sense of time passing. He tried to sleep, but the thought of that pesky rat lurking somewhere in the crypt kept him from any real rest. The once thrilling cat-and-mouse game had become mundane and tedious without his opponent regularly appearing.

As the sounds of men and machines grew louder, Ray's hunger increasingly bothered him, despite the putrid smell surrounding him. The familiar scent of decaying bodies hung in the air, a reminder of his grim situation. The smell of urine lingered in this tomb, though he'd had no recent urge to relieve himself due to dehydration. The dried blood on his clothes irritated his skin with every movement. Despite it all, he found solace in thanking God for even the smallest things, and in counting it all joy, knowing the transformation this situation could yield.

The sudden sight of blood streaming down his face, drenching his scalp, didn't frighten Ray. The bristly tail brushing against the back of his neck, though, that gave him the creeps, and snapped him out of his daze. The creature had perched on top of Ray's head, mistaking him for dead and taking advantage of an easy meal. Ray didn't remember falling asleep, but the fact that Spot had settled on his head and begun gnawing at it suggested he had been motionless for some time. Despite the weight of the six-pound rat, its sharp nails piercing into his skin, the sound of chewing beside his ear, and the tail wrapping around his neck and down to his stomach, Ray did not budge.

Opportunity had presented itself. The only dilemma now concerned how to eliminate the adversary. Ray's wound would heal in minutes. He had only enough time to remain still and calculate the rat's downfall. Surprise would be his biggest weapon, along with his size, strength, and intelligence. He'd use them all.

Ray swiftly grabbed hold of the rat's tail, conveniently within his reach. The mixture of rough bristles and coarse hair protruding from dry, flaky skin repulsed him more than he anticipated. However, he was confident in his advantage.

In one quick motion, he slammed it repeatedly against a large slab of cement. The gruesome mess of blood, human and rodent, splattered all over the cold ground. He reveled in triumph.

Blinding rays of sun burst into his cavern, shining directly into his face. *Is this real, or a figment of my imagination?* Dust and dirt showered down on him, igniting a glimmer of hope in his soul. His eternal optimism as a believer in Jesus sparked anew, the light and noise promising another chance at life.

Meanwhile, Monica comfortably settled into the back of the limousine, slowly making her way to FBO General Aviation Terminal Building 145, the private plane services at JFK Airport. Horace opened Monica's door and assured her he would take care of her suitcases. She took a moment to thank him for the prayers and encouragement.

Once they reached the tarmac, Monica spotted the sleek Gulfstream G55 corporate jet waiting for her, its CCJN logo shining in the sunlight. The door stood open. As she climbed the steps to the plane, a flight attendant greeted her with a sympathetic smile.

Inside, Steve Moore sat with his laptop, live streaming from Cairo through a CCJN satellite connection. He wore headphones, completely absorbed in his work until Monica entered the plane. Hastily removing them as he stood, he embraced her with comforting warmth, like an old friend.

Steve introduced her to the show's producers, Al Coffey and John Miller, as well as their assistant Mark Betts. "Nice to meet you, Mrs. Witt. I'm sorry about your husband," Mark offered somewhat insincerely, like a detached doctor delivering bad news to a family member after they lost a loved one—cold and matter-of-fact.

Steve bore into Mark with a sharp look for his callous remark as he escorted Monica to her seat. "Are you ready?" he asked, then gestured for the attendant, Amber, to close the door.

"More than ready," Monica replied, taking note of the three other passengers already on board the custom craft. Al looked seasoned at fifty, a little overweight with a receding hairline, but had a friendly face full of wisdom. John appeared ambitious and well put together in a new suit, tie, and shoes—all clearly chosen for this adventure. Mark's attire was relaxed, consisting of a sport jacket and polo shirt. He clearly understood his position as an apprentice and assistant to his superiors.

Amber opened the cockpit door and spoke with the flight crew before the custom luxury jet began taxiing down the runway, only minutes after they boarded.

Though her reason for travel was not ideal, Monica couldn't deny the impressiveness of the private jet her first time riding in one. She barely noticed the purring engines as the plane soared through uninterrupted blue skies. The luxurious amenities in its custom interior were top-notch, with large, plush leather seats that enveloped her in comfort, adjacent to elegant red oak end tables. If that wasn't enough, a massive 60-inch TV provided live satellite access to news stations anywhere in the world.

A flight attendant catering to their every need was a luxury reserved for the wealthy and famous, or in this case, the desperate.

"Monica, how are you holding up?" Steve asked casually, trying to gauge her emotional state.

"Honestly, everything is happening so quickly. I haven't had time to process my feelings. Ray's out there somewhere, and all we can do is trust God for the outcome," she replied with a hint of desperation.

"Of course," he replied in his usual direct manner. "Ray is a strong man and he knows how to survive. Let's keep hoping for the best."

"Some hope and some pray," Monica quipped back, catching everyone's attention.

After a long pause, Amber broke the tension. "Is anyone hungry?"

CHAPTER SIX

Old Times

Tanya secretly slid two magazines under her arm before guiding RJ and the massive truck he drove toward the bins. It moved at a snail's pace. The long fork arms scooped up the garbage and lifted it toward the open mouth of the truck dumpster, producing the familiar clattering sound of garbage on garbage. RJ had become skilled enough to navigate out the narrow alley corridors without Tanya's help, so it was no surprise when she hopped in the cab next to him, still visibly upset.

Tanya tucked the magazines into her backpack and gazed straight ahead, silent. They were both grateful for lunchtime, and it seemed best to head to separate restaurants. As they turned the corner, Tanya effortlessly hopped out of the truck with her personal belongings in tow. No need for small talk. "I'll see you in thirty minutes," she called out as she disappeared around the truck.

"Women!" RJ mumbled under his breath, making sure no women could actually hear him.

Tanya was no stranger to keeping secrets; it had been a necessary skill her whole life. She quickly made her way to The Greek Spot. She couldn't wait for the best gyro this side of Greece. Greek food had always been her favorite, no matter where she had lived. As she settled into her favorite booth, the hostess brought over a cool glass of water—more than refreshing, it was delightful. With a collection of magazines and newspaper clippings spread out in front of her, Tanya continued searching for stories of miraculous survivors, ones who had defied all the odds. She eagerly flipped through the pages of her new collection.

Carrie, a familiar waitress, also Tanya's roommate and best friend, interrupted her trance. "Hey girl, what's up?"

"I don't know. What's up with you?" Tanya answered playfully.

"Just working the J-O-B. I can tell you're still on the job too," Carrie remarked while holding her nose. Tanya didn't have a comeback. It's tough to work knee-deep in garbage without smelling like it. "The usual for you?" Carrie asked, already knowing the answer.

"You know it," Tanya replied. "The sooner you bring it, the sooner you can breathe some fresh air." Carrie laughed and disappeared behind the counter to place the order, their banter a testament to their strong friendship and mutual respect.

The headline "Man Survives Bear Attack" immediately caught her attention. The article detailed that he had only sustained minor injuries. She studied his face in a picture intently, trying to remember if she had seen him before. No, he was just a stranger, she hadn't known him in the past, and she had no reason to get to know him in the future.

The next article grabbed her: "Man Survives Gunshot Wound to Head in New York." It explained how a brain injury causes the most deadly type of damage, and it has a high mortality rate. The article highlighted the incredible story of a man who had made a near-complete recovery just one year after being shot. He showed no signs of sensory or motor impairment and had no lasting disabilities. She couldn't believe it! Initially, she believed this was simply another story of a tragic shooting death in New York City. *But he was still alive? Fully recovered?* She eagerly turned the page for more details and pictures, but wound up disappointed. "I've never seen him before," she said aloud.

Moving on, she turned to the next article: "Man Survives Ten Days at Sea with No Food or Water." This one, written fifty years ago, particularly interested her. Tanya thought that she recognized the man in the photos—especially in the sun-dried "after" shot. He was in a different time and place, yet a sense of familiarity washed over her. She fixed on his eyes, windows to the soul. While his other features may have changed, she would always remember those eyes, eerily similar to her own, not in terms of appearance, size, shape, or color, but in what they seemed to hide—a past filled with untold secrets. They sat emotionless and void of any true expression of feeling. "Yes, no doubt about it. I know this man," Tanya muttered under her breath.

Carrie's voice interrupted her thoughts: "You look like you've just seen a ghost."

Tanya gave her a reassuring smile. "I just need some time alone to think," she explained. Carrie nodded understandingly and went back to waitressing. Tanya took a deep breath and let herself drift back into a dreamlike state, where memories overlapped and intermingled with one another.

———————————————————

Time was a blur to Tanya (then known as Kim). The atmosphere held thick layers of panic and terror. People ran in every direction in shock and disbelief. Fires raged, and attempts to put them out seemed futile with such primitive fire equipment. Bodies lay unidentifiable amongst mangled metal debris, waiting for confirmation of their identities. Media outlets had just released news of the devastating *Hindenburg* air disaster.

The date sits etched in history: May 6, 1937, at the Lakehurst Naval Air Station in New Jersey, when a single spark ignited the outer cover of the *Hindenburg*. In just thirty-four seconds, flames engulfed the entire airship. It reminded Kim of another tragic incident on January 28, 1986: the explosion of the space shuttle *Challenger* on that clear day over the Atlantic, near Florida. Although Kim wasn't physically present that day, she was alive. Yet she saw no point in scrutinizing the event. Her search would not be fruitful there—too few people and too much public attention for the individuals she sought. It only connected to her because the tragedy occurred in U.S. airspace, with lives lost and horrifying footage and commentary.

Kim tirelessly searched her memories for those who had survived the *Hindenburg* disaster beyond reason, the ones who shouldn't have made it out alive but did. Her mission? Find those miraculous cases, those left untouched in a tragedy that claimed large loss of lives. She wasn't interested in the visibly injured or damaged; she sought out those with invisible scars and healed wounds, who seemed out of place among the chaos of those searching for their loved ones on that fateful flight. It presented her with a daunting task, especially at night, the dim light offering only faint images projected by lanterns and torches that guided her way. But Kim pressed on, determined to remember even a few faces for future reference. She would return in the morning and spend the entire day at the crash site, if necessary, just to remember those she saw tonight.

In her mind, she quietly walked away from the scene, unnoticed but not uncaring, heart full of compassion for what she had witnessed. She knew this was just one more chapter in her search. Tomorrow would bring new hope, new possibilities, and she would continue her quest until she accounted for everyone. Until tomorrow, until tomorrow . . .

Tanya snapped out of her daydream and lifted her gaze from the magazine in front of her. Carrie stood above her with a concerned expression. "Hey there, are you doing okay?"

Tanya's mind quickly shifted to the present. "Yes, I'm fine," she replied, with the image of the man and the '37 disaster still lingering in her thoughts.

"Great, here's your gyro with seasoned fries, and I also brought you a new menu item to try—baklava! Thought you might like it." With a parting smile, Carrie headed off to attend to other customers.

Tanya quickly reopened the article, her interest not in reading but in studying the face of the man pictured there. She observed the features behind his sunburnt, cracked skin. He definitely appeared Jewish. While she didn't have "typical" Jewish features, this man seemed to fit the stereotype perfectly. Tanya felt a twinge of guilt at profiling him, but she couldn't help noticing his Mediterranean features: dark hair, olive skin, and intense dark eyes with heavy eyebrows. *Does it count as racism when you're thinking about your own people?* she pondered.

She polished off her gyro and fries first, savoring every bite before moving on to the baklava. She couldn't resist pausing to appreciate the delicious flavor. A sip of Mom & Pop's root beer added the perfect finish to her lunch.

As she headed for the exit, Carrie chastised her for leaving newspapers and magazines on the table for her to clean up. Tanya didn't care about any of those other publications; she only cared about the one clutched tightly under her arm. "You ain't right!" Carrie exclaimed as Tanya breezed out the door.

"Mind your business," Tanya retorted with a side smile, turning back for the last word.

Tanya's preoccupation with the article and the short exchange with Carrie took her mind off the short space between the building and the road. She stepped into the rushing New York street without looking. The screeching of a truck rose above the usual sounds of traffic as it hurled Tanya and her prized magazine through the air. The moment seemed endless before both crashed onto the unforgiving pavement. *Seems like old times*, Tanya painfully reflected as she lay there.

CHAPTER SEVEN

Rescued

The echoing clanks of machinery rang in Ray's ears; vibrations of heavy equipment moving giant cinder blocks above him rumbled through his body. Dirt and dust particles rained down on his face. "Hey! I'm down here!" he yelled out, but the deafening noise drowned out his cries. As he looked around, Ray knew that one wrong move could cause the massive columns of cement to shift and crush him. Despite this danger, he knew any injury would eventually heal. The explanation for his rapid healing worried him more.

As debris continued flooding the space, Ray cried out, "Lord, I need you! You have helped me so many times in crisis—I know you hear me now. Please rescue me!" At that moment, the earth beneath Ray shifted, moving slabs of concrete above him and creating a small chasm to his left and right. The showering debris fell around Ray, as the slabs created an umbrella over his body. This wasn't luck, chance, or a result of the workers above him, but a direct and immediate answer to prayer. "Thank you, Lord. Thank you!"

Perhaps it was his career as a journalist, or maybe his survival instincts simply kicked in: Ray quickly tore off the remnants of his shirt, then scoured the new cavern for a suitable pole. The chances of finding one amidst the rubble of a collapsed building seemed slim, but God was on his side. He fumbled upon a twelve-foot wrought iron pole that had likely been used during construction of the now-ruined tower. Bits of cement were attached to it, but with some determination and clever thinking, he could make it work. He began breaking off pieces of cement until the pole became smooth enough to work with, then he tied his torn shirt to one end. Determined, he navigated through the darkness toward patches of light.

Pushing, twisting, and shaking the pole with all his might into the debris above, he felt the shaft break open. *Finally!* He exclaimed. He stretched hard, fully extending the pole above his head, but maneuvering it so the flag was visible challenged him.

I've come this far. I'm not gonna let this small obstacle stop me. Ray had a life he had learned to love, with an ambitious, beautiful wife who loved him like no other ever had. Sharing a home in New York City with Monica, enjoying life with good friends and a job that took him all over the world. *No way I'm staying here!* Who would want to lie in the putrid ruins of a building indefinitely? The constant smell of damp cement, urine, and death, along with the dry air, isolation, and utter darkness wore on him. Spot had provided some relief from the monotony, but not the positive kind.

Again, using a nearby rock for leverage, he managed to shake the rod around until the flag rose above the rubble. With more dust and dirt pouring into the cavern as heavy machinery closed in on his position, the urgency of the situation was apparent.

Then, suddenly, everything came to a halt. *"Marhaban,"* echoed into the cavern, a common Arabic greeting. Then, *"As-salamu alaykum"*—"Peace be upon you." A friendly voice pierced through the darkness, giving Ray a glimmer of hope.

He shouted out desperately, "Help! I'm down here!" In a burst of movement and noise, he kicked and shook the makeshift flagpole in hopes of capturing anyone's attention.

Tap, tap, tap, the pole reverberated. Without hesitation, he grabbed a rock and tapped back in response. It had been years since he last used Morse code, but at this point, he was willing to try anything. Four short taps followed by one tap, then three short and one long tap—he sent out the message rhythmically on the pole. To his relief, an understandable pattern came back in response. "I'm down here!" Ray yelled at the top of his lungs, hoping the person above would hear him.

He sat down, watching as chunks of concrete carefully disappeared above him. His mind raced, trying to invent an explanation for how he had survived this ordeal. There would be no easy way to do it. He could try to run away as soon as the opening was large enough to escape, but where would he go? He had no place in Egypt to hide or blend in. Historically, Jews and Egyptians were not on good terms; in fact, they were often hostile toward each other. With his Jewish heritage, running wasn't a viable option.

A goatskin canteen flew down and landed beside him, breaking his train of thought, followed by a bag containing three protein bars. As he reached for it, he realized how incredibly thirsty he was, waiting so many days without water. Normally he only drank bottled water, but in his current state, that didn't even cross his mind. He chugged down the life-saving liquid.

Looking up, he saw hues of dusk painting the sky. *Will the rescue team get me out of here tonight?* A bright spotlight shone through the wreckage into the cavern. "Hey, is there an American down there?" a booming voice echoed through the shaft.

"Yes!" Ray responded eagerly.

"Don't worry, we'll have you out by morning," the voice reassured him. "We have a doctor up here who would like to measure your vitals with a monitor. Can we lower it down and see if you need immediate medical attention? Can you hook it up to yourself?"

Ray faced another dilemma: His vitals would read "normal." Other than fatigue, he actually felt pretty good. "What did you say? It's hard to hear you," he replied. The voice repeated the message loudly and clearly, this time with a bull horn. "No, no, I don't have enough room to hook up a monitor, and I don't know how!" Ray said, trying to buy more time.

"Okay, we'll continue to slowly remove the area around you," the voice said in broken English.

"Okay, thank you. Thank you!" Ray shouted back, settling himself on the rocks and contemplating his return to civilization.

CHAPTER EIGHT

By Grace

Funny thing is, when you believe you are going to die, random thoughts and questions flood your mind: *How did this happen? What will become of me? Is this really happening?* Your life doesn't play out like a movie montage—sheer panic, fear, and the continual consideration of eternity engulf you. Although he had faced death many times, Tony never got used to it. *Is this one the final, true death for me?* he wondered.

As the engine roared in his ears, Tony marveled at its perfectly tuned mechanics. *Ironic that I'd evaluate the engine about to engulf me.*

Fred liked being in the captain's seat. Grabbing the yoke, feet on the rudder pedals, he imagined himself soaring at 40,000 feet. The hum of the engine below contributed to the fantasy. Feeling the phone vibrate in his pocket he saw a couple of Instagram messages, so he mocked putting the plane on autopilot and answered them, oblivious to the plight of his boss below.

No claw marks etched into the smooth metal frame, too polished for any signs of struggle. Only the silent screams of a doomed man echoed in his ears as his denim uniform tore apart and massive blades crushed his bones.

His ankles, then knees, everything followed its proper sequence. Most people wouldn't remember the details of death in such clarity, but Tony did.

He recalled the strange sensation of his hip bones shifting and the soft tissue of his ribs turn to mush. Instinctively, he wanted to duck and cover his head, but it seemed futile in the face of a jet engine.

Even in moments like this, grace and miracles happen.

In the blink of an eye, the massive engine spit Tony out the back and onto the floor. After only a few seconds in the turbines, his body lay crushed and unrecognizable on the ground, his mind barely conscious, unable to comprehend the situation. He felt like a tree branch fed through a shredder. But even in this shattered state, he could feel his bones realigning and flesh merging, like a skilled surgeon carefully reconnecting the veins, arteries, and tendons in an accident victim. Tony thought of it more like God meticulously knitting together a baby in a mother's womb in a matter of seconds. Blood rushed through empty vessels and physical functions returned to normal. His heart beat strongly, lungs filled with oxygen, and brain fired signals to every part of his body in perfect harmony.

No one could possibly understand the feeling of physical death and resurrection, yet it was all too familiar to him, regardless how surreal the experience. At least that's what he thought. He lay there gasping for air, and couldn't believe he had been given yet another chance at life. A fifth chance, maybe more. He had lost count.

He worried less about his own survival and more about explaining how he had managed to make it through an engine turbine unscathed. Anyone else would surely have perished, permanently. Truth is, he had been through countless near-death experiences—facing lions in the Roman arena, engaging in bloody battles in the Crusades, watching his friend Joan of Arc's execution, and even journeying to America for the Louisiana Purchase negotiations. With Spain, the United States, and France vying for control of the Mississippi River, trouble popped up around every bend. Yet he always remembered . . . everything.

As Tony surveyed his injuries, he noticed his shirt had been torn to shreds, leaving his wounds exposed. The sight of the mixture of blood, flesh, and hair unsettled him. *Can I still walk? Or run?* he questioned as he checked his legs and lower torso for any serious damage. Thankfully, he could do both. With a renewed sense of hope, he searched for a safe place to rest and recover. He spotted some large boxes near the tail section of the L-1011 aircraft and ambled over there undetected, relying predominantly on his most-healed leg.

Tony didn't believe in luck or karma when it came to surviving life-threatening situations. This wasn't a matter of chance or fate, but the protection of God Almighty. As a child, he was raised in the traditional teachings of Judaism that focused on the Torah, the first five books of the Hebrew Bible. As a grown man, he considered himself a practicing Jew, participating in most Jewish customs and rituals. Even after centuries had passed, he still held on to the wisdom and teachings from studying the writings of King David and other biblical Hebrew writers as a young boy.

Resting in his hidden refuge, Tony's injuries had nearly healed. *I just need another ten minutes,* he whispered to himself. He heard the engines power down. The familiar sound of alloy and aluminum whistling through the thin air of the hangar brought him comfort. Feeling unexpectedly exhausted, his head hit the ground, and he fell into a deep sleep.

After answering his Instagram messages, Fred returned from his state of reverie. Pushing the intercom on his headset, he checked in with Tony. "Boss, what is the status of the panel? Are we ready to power down?" Fred repeated the message, with no reply. A third time, he transmitted the message. Silence. Panic washed over him as he climbed into the copilot's seat to look down at the engine. "Powering down . . . powering down!" he cried as he cut off the fuel supply, then turned off the ignition.

Fred jumped down from the plane and frantically searched the hangar, finally locating Tony. "Boss, are you okay?" Freddie shook him hard.

"What? Who?" Tony mumbled, slowly emerging from his unconsciousness. He had no idea how long he had been asleep. He lay shirtless on the floor, pants ripped and tattered. One shoe remained in place, while the other was missing, along with his sock. *This is going to be a disaster.* "Stop shaking me, Freddie! Don't you realize that shaking an injured person is the last thing you should do?"

"I'm sorry. When I saw all the blood on the right inlet and compressor, I was afraid something happened to you. I followed the trail and found you here."

"Calm down," Tony said, trying to stall and concoct a believable explanation. "Can you help me up? I was just checking the module in sector R26. Did you start the engine?" Even as he asked the question, he already knew the answer—Freddie had definitely started it. But he needed more time to clear his head and come up with a plausible explanation for what had just happened.

"Yes, boss, I started it." Freddie quickly responded.

Trying to play it cool, Tony played along. "I must have been thrown out somehow. My head hurts like crazy." This was partly true; he did have a headache from hitting his head during the incident.

"There's so much blood!" Freddie exclaimed. "But you don't even have a scratch!"

Tony remained silent as he took a moment to gather his thoughts. Slowly they walked out from the crates into the center of the hangar. "I don't remember anything, but I suppose it's a good thing I'm not injured," he replied.

"Well, yeah, of course," Freddie said with a hint of uncertainty.

"Take the rest of the day off, Freddie. You need it," Tony said as they made their way toward the locker room. He paused in front of the aircraft while Freddie walked on, then pointed up at the silent turbo engine. "Not this time . . . Not this time."

Another wonder had unfolded before him—a fresh start, a new beginning, and the sweet joy of living again. His triumphant journey—from death to resurrection!

CHAPTER NINE

Do You Believe in Miracles?

According to the watch Ray had gifted her on their ten-year anniversary, Monica had been on the ground exactly 53 hours, 29 minutes, and 45 seconds. The watch held special memories for her, such as warm Acapulco nights on the beach with the love of her life. But even as she reminisced, she could hear the loud hum of machinery outside her hotel room. The nonstop excavation to clear the earthquake and building damage was a constant reminder of the devastation surrounding her. The air was thick with dust, dirt, and death, a grim reality she couldn't escape.

The knock on her door barely registered in Monica's mind. "Maid service," a voice announced, struggling with English. It was definitely time for fresh towels and toiletries, and clean bedding. The four half-eaten trays on her nightstand were evidence of being holed up in her room for two-plus days. "Just a second," she replied as she hastily threw on her robe and slippers, fumbling with the security latch before opening the door.

She looked a bit ruffled, with tousled hair and face devoid of any makeup, at least she thought so. *Did I even bring my makeup?* she wondered, in a half-daze. *I can't remember.* As the maid cleaned the hotel room, she stepped out onto the balcony to take in the view. *Just as it seemed from my room.* She closed her eyes and prayed. *God, why am I here?* then cried out loud, overwhelmed. *Why do you seem so far away? Have you abandoned me? Am I alone in all this?*

The sound of the muezzin's call to prayer echoed from a nearby minaret, startling Monica. The irony struck her: At that very moment, she was praying to God, while the Muslims were praying to an idea they could never know. Her perspective shifted and realigned; she stopped questioning. "God, You are all-knowing, and Your will and ways are perfect. I know in my heart You have me and Ray covered, both now and forever. Please forgive my lack of faith."

"Ma'am, I'm finished," a voice informed her from the other room. The difference in cleanliness was striking—her life had fallen into disarray in only a few days. She made the decision: *It's time to change things.* As she headed toward the bathroom for a shower, the phone rang.

Steve's voice on the other end caught her off guard. "Can you be ready in an hour? We want to send a car for you."

"Absolutely," she answered. Before she could ask why, he hung up.

A million thoughts raced through her mind as she showered, sat at her makeup table, and stood in front of her closet. *I'll go with the dark blue pantsuit*, she decided, not wanting to wear all black. That color seemed too somber, too much a representation of grief, and she needed faith that Ray was still alive. As she slipped into the rest of her outfit, she reminded herself again and again, *He is alive.* Her hour was almost up, but punctuality wasn't very important in Egypt. She took her time.

As she returned to the bedroom area, the blinking light on the phone grabbed her attention. She hadn't heard it ring. "Hello?" she answered, waiting for a response.

"Good day, ma'am. Your car has arrived," the hotel receptionist announced.

"I'll be right down," she replied, hanging up and quickly heading downstairs. As she made her way through the grand entrance into the lobby, she took in the stunning beauty of the marble floors carved with intricate Egyptian patterns. Images of King Tut topped golden columns, while lions adorned fountains and human busts decorated the majestic atmosphere. The water and lights created a perfect blend of ancient elegance and modern architecture. Bellhops, desk personnel, and other staff wore uniforms perfectly matching the decor. The brief interlude of beauty and order created a welcome distraction from the heavy burden she carried.

A slender Egyptian gentleman seemed to recognize Monica as he held the car door open for her. She settled into the limo, full of familiar faces: Steve Moore, Al Coffey, John Miller, and Mark Betts. Like déjà vu. Before anyone else could greet her, Steve offered a simple "Hello, Monica." The rest of the group acknowledged her presence with a nod. As they drove away, Monica picked up the scent of alcohol, something she was acutely attuned to since she didn't drink much herself. *It seems a little early in the day to be drinking.*

Steve continued. "Monica, we're heading to the hotel where Ray was last seen. From there, we'll figure out our next move." She couldn't help but find his phrasing odd. "It's not too far from your hotel," he added, as if he had memorized each word beforehand.

She kept silent during the car ride. The foursome weren't her favorite people on the plane, and that fact remained true here. *Here we go, Lord. I'll roll with whatever happens next.*

The upheaval made the city and roads unrecognizable—a far cry from their normal state—busy with bumper-to-bumper traffic, horns honking, and people filling the streets. Everywhere she looked, Monica saw remnants of the disaster that had struck this ancient city. Buildings were reduced to rubble, and streets split by deep crevices separated entire neighborhoods. Since her flight had arrived in the early hours of the morning, she hadn't seen the full extent of the destruction. With jet lag, she'd slept during the short commute from the airport to the hotel. As she looked around at the despair and devastation, she couldn't help but feel guilty being so consumed with her own problems. In this overpopulated city, millions were either dead, missing, or struggling to find food and shelter. How could she be so self-absorbed about Ray when so many others were suffering?

The car made a final turn past the Cairo Tower, which now leaned lopsided like the Tower of Pisa. They had reached their destination. As the group exited the vehicle, they realized something clearly significant was happening, and they were met with utter chaos. People frantically ran in all directions, shouting, holding their heads or falling to their knees and crying out to Allah. They had no idea what had caused such commotion. Steve grabbed hold of the driver and demanded answers, shaking him as he spoke. "What's going on? What's happening?"

"I have no idea, sir!" he responded in panic. He pointed to the right. "Try getting to the building with the big crane and crowds."

Mark, the youngest of the group, eagerly pulled out his camera and began recording as he ran toward the commotion. The others followed as fast as they could, with the driver trailing behind. An ambulance, police, and rescue personnel had already populated the scene. Flashing blue and red lights warned bystanders to keep their distance. A frenzied crowd had already gathered around a gurney; people forcefully pushed and shoved each other. Al and John, the two older men, avoided the chaos by slowly bringing up the rear of the group.

"Man alive!" the driver shouted, as he reached the edge of the crowd.

"What?" Steve and Monica shouted in unison.

"Look, over there," the driver replied, pointing toward the ambulance. Mark returned from that direction, breaking through the crowd to reach them, pale and shocked. He fell to his knees, camera still in hand.

Steve and Monica caught up to him. "What happened? What did you see?" Steve asked frantically. Monica had never seen Steve so agitated. Still hunched over, Mark's weak and trembling voice replied, "It . . . It's Ray."

Breaking away, Monica ran toward the back of the ambulance. The two men attending to Ray's vital signs were taken aback by her sudden appearance as she pushed through the crowd. During the chaos and noise of unfamiliar languages, Monica called out for Ray. He recognized her voice and managed to sit up, unstrapping himself from the gurney. "Let her pass!" he demanded, swinging his legs over the edge of the stretcher. "Monica! I'm here!" Ray shouted, pushing aside the medical workers in the way. He didn't consider his smell after being trapped under rubble for so many days; it only mattered that he was alive, and the woman he loved was calling out to him. Despite her desperation, her voice sounded like music to his ears.

The crowd erupted into applause and cheers as the couple wrapped their arms around each other. Love truly is universal. Mark made his way back through the crowd, composed, and began recording the emotional reunion. "I love you, Ray," Monica cried. "I was so scared of losing you."

"That will never happen, babe," Ray replied. Despite the hunger and thirst, he knew he was perfectly healthy. He felt the attendant pull at his arm, trying to guide him back to the gurney. But Monica was determined to stay with him. She turned toward Steve and yelled over the cheers, "I'm going with Ray!" Steve acknowledged her with a nod and wave. The paramedics loaded Ray into the back of the vehicle and Monica jumped in, moving the attendant to the side. As the ambulance inched its way through the cheering crowd, she held on to Ray's hand tightly.

Watching the ambulance roll off, Steve faced his colleagues. "What the hell just happened?"

Their puzzled expressions provided no answers.

The next day the trio returned to the earthquake scene and picked up right where they left off. "Mark," Steve inquired, "what room and floor was Ray on?"

Mark rummaged through papers stuffed in his back pocket. He scrolled through the list with his finger. "Room 4202, sir, on the 42nd floor."

Steve's gaze shifted toward the wreckage of the St. Regis Hotel, once a grand building, now a chaotic mess of broken beams. "How?" he muttered. "How could anyone survive a fall like that?" He turned back to his team, seeking answers.

No one wanted to speculate, but Al tentatively suggested, "Perhaps he was in an elevator or staircase when the earthquake hit."

John nodded in agreement. "That's possible." Their journalistic instincts kicked into high gear. "Maybe he was on the first floor or outside," he added. Mark remained quiet, not wanting to interrupt.

"What?!" Steve exclaimed, "If that's true, the building would have landed right on top of him! Look at the way it collapsed inward before toppling over."

"True," Al pointed out, rubbing his chin in thought.

"Come on, Al, what do you make of all this?" John asked.

"I don't know much about structural engineering," Al replied honestly. "I'd rather gather facts before jumping to any conclusions."

As they made their way toward the ruins of an older building, Steve called for Ahmed, their company interpreter, to join them. "Ahmed, find someone who knows about the construction and architecture of this place," Steve ordered.

"Yes, sir!" Ahmed replied before hurrying off toward construction workers in white helmets.

"We only have a few days left here, and I want some answers before we head back home," Steve stated to no one in particular. Al walked alongside him while Mark continued documenting the remains of the building and its surroundings. He didn't mind keeping his distance from Steve, who was clearly in boss mode.

Ahmed soon reappeared, accompanied by two men wearing suits and white construction helmets. "Sir, this is Bassel Naguib and Geb Rami, both trained at American universities and fluent in English. They should be able to address your inquiries."

Bassel greeted Steve and Al with a handshake. Al reciprocated the gesture. "Nice to meet you," he offered.

Steve pointed toward the rubble of the building. "We have some questions about that structure and the earthquake."

Geb nodded. "We will assist if possible." Bassel added, "Currently, we are in the early stages of our investigation of not only that building, but various structures throughout the city." Geb chimed in: "It will take years of work and effort to fully comprehend the extent of the damage."

"Thank you for taking the time to inform us about this hotel," Al replied.

Bassel commented, "This was once one of the most magnificent structures in all of Egypt, an architectural marvel."

Steve, intrigued, asked, "What made it so special?"

Geb replied with a somber tone, "Not only was it visually stunning, it was designed to withstand an earthquake with a magnitude of 8.0 or even 9.0." Gesturing toward some debris, he continued, "However, as you can see here, the building next door collapsed onto this one during the quake." Bassel added, "If you look around, you can see how the buildings cascaded like dominoes."

"I do apologize for interrupting," Steve interjected. "But could you please show us where our employee was rescued from the debris? I'm curious about how he managed to survive amidst such destruction."

Bassel and Geb abruptly broke away from the group without a word and began conversing in hushed tones. The CCJN team exchanged wondering glances, while Ahmed threw his hands up in surprise.

The two men rejoined the group, and Bassel stated firmly, "Gentlemen, we are not at liberty to speculate on how your man could have possibly survived down there for an extended period of time. Neither of us have personally examined the area, but we have been informed that a hollow cavern exists where someone could have potentially lived."

Steve and Al immediately sensed they were either lying or withholding information, so they directly questioned the two men. "Were there any other bodies found near Ray's location?" Al inquired.

"Yes," Bassel replied, "actually a large number of bodies, like a mass grave. We are uncovering more every day." Geb shot Bassel a disapproving look for his hasty response.

Steve spoke up, attempting to change the subject. "Can we visit the site and see for ourselves?"

"Oh no," Bassel exclaimed, "only authorized individuals are permitted beyond this point."

As the group continued speculating, Mark wandered toward the rescue site, capturing footage of the entire area as he climbed over concrete slabs and barbed wire to reach the location the men were discussing. Suddenly, a man's voice boomed from a crane in Arabic. Bassel and Geb turned toward Mark, filming in the restricted area. "Get out of there!" they yelled as he continued to advance toward the forbidden section of the wreckage. Undeterred, he paused and zoomed in on the cavern's entrance, capturing as much footage as possible before several men in red hats arrived and removed him from the area.

As he tried to return to his colleagues, a group of soldiers in military uniforms stepped in his path to stop him. Ahmed and his team quickly ran toward them. The military police were yelling and pointing at Mark, then took hold of his arms to escort him to a military jeep.

Steve asked loudly, "What's going on here?"

Geb responded, "They want to arrest your cameraman for filming in the restricted area." The police had already taken away Mark's camera.

Steve turned to Ahmed and the other leaders. "Is there anything we can do?"

Bassel replied sternly, "After suffering great loss in our community, you and your colleague have shown disrespect by entering this restricted area and filming without permission. Now you expect us to help you?"

Steve apologized. "We meant no disrespect, but as journalists, we sometimes get carried away in pursuit of a story." Geb and Bassel huddled briefly before approaching the police officers. Steve and Al stood nearby, unable to understand the conversation but waiting anxiously for an answer.

Ahmed returned with Geb and Bassel to relay the news. "They'll release your friend, but they want to keep the camera," he said. "That's the only way they'll let him go and allow us to leave without further issue."

Steve and Al exchanged looks. Steve asked, "Can't they just take the tape? That camera is expensive!"

"He should have thought of that before entering a restricted area," Bassel remarked.

"Ultimately, getting our teammate back is more important than the camera," Al added.

Geb spoke up. "We will inform them of your decision." Steve and Al turned away, disappointed.

Before leaving, Bassel turned and chastised them. "This is why we left the United States—because you have no respect and can't follow simple rules. Why must you always be the ugly Americans?"

On their way back to the limousine, Steve leaned in toward Mark. "What did you see down that hole? What was so important they would risk causing an international incident by detaining an American journalist?"

Mark suddenly stopped, overcome, and tears streamed down his face. His words choked out with emotion as he recalled the horrific scene. "I will never forget what I saw down there . . . It was like a mass grave from a Nazi concentration camp." He paused, breathing in deep before continuing. "Only these people weren't the victims of genocide, but an earthquake. Men, women, and children, dead and mangled, right where they were when disaster struck."

Steve's confusion heightened. "How could Ray have survived that?"

Mark shook his head, still in disbelief. "I didn't see a single scratch on him; it just doesn't make sense."

Their conversation continued with no clear solution in sight. Steve finally turned to Mark and posed the question, "What do you think?"

Mark paused. "Do you believe in miracles?"

CHAPTER TEN

Still Rolling

Tanya remained sprawled out on the unforgiving, parched concrete as her eyes darted around in panic. She was too preoccupied with finding her lost magazine to acknowledge the pain radiating through her body. A group of concerned bystanders started to gather, bombarding her with questions.

A middle-aged woman broke through the circle. "I'm Lynda. I'm a nurse. Are you okay?" she asked Tanya, grasping her wrist to check it for a pulse. Another bystander shouted, "Someone call 9-1-1!"

Tanya actually wanted everyone to disappear. She knew nothing would come from the mishap. *No doubt, I'm walking out of here,* she thought confidently.

Amidst the crowd of the looky loos a man's voice rang out in distress. "She came out of nowhere . . . I couldn't stop! It's not my fault!"

He seems more troubled by the accident than me, Tanya thought. She saw the truck driver in overalls, holding his head desperately and searching for someone, anyone, who would understand.

Unexpectedly, a police officer pushed through the crowd and yelled, "Back up, everyone . . . Give her some room!"

Tanya went along with it. "Yeah, give me some space."

Another person held Tanya's hand. She looked up and realized it was Carrie. Despite the pain and tears etched on Carrie's face, it brought Tanya comfort to see her good friend. "How are you?" Carrie asked, forcing a smile.

Tanya reciprocated with her own forced smile. "I don't think I'm quite ready for another gyro."

The officer leaned closer and asked, "Miss, do you need medical assistance? The ambulance is on its way."

Tanya shook her head and replied firmly, "I don't need one."

"What's your name?" the man in blue asked.

Tanya promptly answered with a hint of attitude, "Tanya Bloom, residing at 10168 King Street in Manhattan's West Village." She displayed her signature sass even while lying wounded in a gutter.

Tanya could hear the low moan of the ambulance approaching. *Oh no*, she thought. *I have to get back to work.* Even more important than that, she wanted to locate the magazine. "Carrie, do you see my magazine?" Tanya asked.

"What an odd question!" Carrie wondered aloud. "What, Tanya?"

"Where is my magazine from the restaurant?" Tanya repeated, frustration growing.

Carrie turned toward the officer, "She's alright!" then back to Tanya. "Are you kidding me? You're seriously laying here on the ground after getting hit by a truck and your biggest concern is a stupid magazine? Are you for real?" Carrie exclaimed, turning to the onlookers. With a heavy dose of sarcasm, she added, "Did anyone happen to see a *magazine* lying around? My best friend dropped it when she was *hit by a truck!* Anyone? No one?" She spun around in frustration looking back at her friend.

Unbelievably, a young boy spoke up in a small, meek voice. "I found an old magazine."

Tanya sat up, pushing away the hands trying to hold her down. "Let me see," she demanded, motioning for him to come closer. The crowd slowly parted, revealing a boy around thirteen or fourteen years old. Tanya reached out her bloody, scratched-up hand for the magazine. The officer nodded in affirmation to the boy to approach, who seemed reluctant in the face of the officer's uniform, gun, and badge.

Without a word, he handed Tanya the magazine. She gazed into his eyes and expressed her gratitude for the cherished item. He scurried away to the opposite side of the crowd. "Come here, son," called the officer with a mix of passion and authority, but too late; he had stealthily vanished into the growing crowd, using his speed to disappear.

"Praise God," Tanya exclaimed as she held on to the magazine. This gentle display of emotion surprised those standing nearby. Amidst the chaos, Tanya clung as tightly as she could to the periodical she had been desperately seeking.

As the paramedics strapped her onto the stretcher, she tightly grasped the magazine, ignoring their request to let it go. Inside the emergency vehicle, the once barely audible siren now served an ear-splitting warning to other drivers on the busy New York streets. With an IV in her arm and various monitors tracking her vital signs, Tanya lay there, longing for peace and quiet.

"What is your name?" the female paramedic asked as her partner sped down the busy avenues. "My name is Maggie," she added, not waiting for Tanya to respond. "Does this hurt?" She pointed to Tanya's arm, clearly dislocated at the elbow.

Tanya resisted sarcastically saying, "What do you think?" then simply replied, "Yes."

"I am going to put it back in place now, Tanya," Maggie continued. "The longer we wait the more it will hurt. Are you ready?" Tanya nodded. "One, two, three!" Maggie effortlessly pushed the elbow back into place. Tanya knew her self-healing abilities were as much responsible for the ease of the movement as the skill of her attendant. "I'll immobilize your arm until we can get it x-rayed at the hospital. You're a real trooper; most people would have freaked out or needed anesthesia for that, but you barely moved," Maggie complimented her.

"I guess I'm still in shock," Tanya offered, not wanting to discuss it further.

"Your vitals and blood pressure are completely normal. They didn't change a bit before, during, or after I snapped your arm into place," Maggie noted, a confused expression on her face.

"Since you don't know me, I wouldn't think too much about it," Tanya suggested. "Can I just rest while you do what needs to be done?"

"Of course," Maggie agreed, wondering how much of what just occurred she wanted to record in her report.

Tanya tightly gripped the magazine with her one good arm, still convinced that she had moved closer to uncovering a mystery of her life that had eluded her for years. She had determined to leave the hospital before even entering it, and notified her boss of this during transport. He promised to inform her partner, RJ, about her mishap. Despite her strong desire to remove the IV needle from her arm before the wound healed, she decided against it, and eventually drifted off to sleep.

The emergency vehicle slowly backed into the bay, its lights flashing as staff members dressed in white eagerly awaited their arrival. The back doors flew open and the team, all wearing masks, rushed Tanya into an already bustling hospital room. She felt the urge to get up and run away before they could do anything to her. But she knew it was pointless—Carrie had given them her address and phone number, it was the only thing that stopped her from fleeing. Here we go, she thought to herself.

"Are you feeling any pain, ma'am?" a nurse inquired. "No," Tanya replied sharply. "Okay, I need to take your vitals," she said as she wrapped a band around Tanya's muscular arm. A device on Tanya's index finger was already pulsating, measuring her oxygen levels.

Another masked individual entered the cubicle. Nurse Holmes reported, "Doctor, a truck hit this woman in midtown Manhattan." The woman pressed a stethoscope against Tanya's chest.

"Please try to remain still," came the voice behind the mask. Tanya noticed the doctor's accent and thick eyebrows. She delivered her directive firmly, yet kindly. "Blood pressure is 110/68, pulse and respiration are normal." After reading through Tanya's chart, she greeted her. "Hello Tanya. I'm Dr. Abrams. Can I check you for any injuries?"

"I feel fine, but go ahead and check," Tanya replied.

"Do you recall being hit?" Dr. Abrams asked as she examined her for any visible injuries.

Tanya knew she had to be clear, concise, and sweet to be released. The first two would be easy, but the last one, That'd require some effort. "Yes, doctor, I remember it vividly," she replied while holding up the magazine as evidence. "I was leaving the restaurant, reading this magazine, and I wasn't paying attention. I walked right into the street."

"Continue," the doctor prompted.

"I was struck by a five-ton GMC truck as I stepped off the curb. At the last second, I saw it coming and braced myself for impact," she lied. "Luckily, I think I managed to spin away from the full impact, which saved me."

Tanya was fully engrossed in her embellished story, completely unaware that Officer Hamilton, from the accident scene, stood directly across the room from the doctor. Tanya jumped when she heard his loud voice interrupting: "Doctor, can I speak with you outside?"

"Certainly, officer," Dr. Abrams replied as they both left the room.

Tanya found herself alone, wondering about the secretive manner of their conversation. This can't be good, she thought. She became aware of pain in her arm from the IV. She knew what was causing it—the puncture mark had already healed thirty or forty minutes post-accident, and her body was rejecting the needle. She carefully removed the syringe from her arm and reinserted it in a new spot nearby, hoping it would last until she could leave. Being me is never easy, she thought as she reclined on the bed once again.

Dr. Abrams noted the officer's name tag. "Yes, Officer Hamilton? What is it?"

"Well, doctor," he said tentatively, pulling out his incident book. "I have multiple witness statements claiming that little lady in there walked directly in front of that truck. It threw her over thirty feet before she landed on the pavement. I don't know if she sustained any brain injuries or if she is simply lying, but she should be severely injured."

Dr. Abrams listened as she fidgeted with her necklace.

"I'll need to file my report soon, so could I speak with her for a moment?" Officer Hamilton asked.

"Physically, she appears to be in perfect condition, so I don't see why you can't talk to her," the doctor replied.

As they entered the room, they saw Tanya sitting up, ready to leave. "I have a few questions for you," Officer Hamilton began. "Do you want to press charges against the truck driver?"

"Absolutely not," came Tanya's quick response. "It wasn't that man's fault, it was mine. I just want to forget about the whole thing," she said as she flipped through her magazine.

"Well, that is your decision," the officer replied. "But I am curious. What was so interesting in that magazine that made you walk out into the middle of the street?"

Tanya thought aloud, "I didn't walk into the middle of the street. I barely made it off the curb." She continued, "I've been searching everywhere for this edition of Newspeak, and I finally found it. I'm a collector."

A little frustrated, the police officer closed his notepad, outsmarted by the woman. "We know where to find you if there are any further questions," he said dismissively as he left the room.

This left the doctor and Tanya alone. "You want to leave, don't you?" Dr. Abrams asked.

"One hundred percent," Tanya replied firmly.

"Well, I don't see any medical reason to keep you here. Your physical exam shows no signs of internal injury, and your cognitive functions appear normal. However, I will sign your release papers if you truthfully answer one question," the doctor insisted.

"I have been an ER doctor about seven years, and I've seen everything in that time; that is, until you walked in. Your clothes are stained with evidence of trauma—cuts, bruises, and scrapes that should have left marks on your skin.

But upon examination, there isn't a scratch to be seen. Even more perplexing is the dry blood on your scalp with no apparent wound. And what amazed me most was how quickly your skin healed around the needle from the IV. It's clear you must have moved it at some point. So, who are you and how is any of this possible?"

I'm caught. Should I run? Then it occurred to her. "Doctor, you asked two questions, so I'll answer the first one." She took a moment to gather her thoughts. "I'm just a simple Jewish girl living in this big city, trying to make a living. I don't think I'm anyone special, just lucky, I guess."

After a brief moment of silence, Dr. Abrams responded simply, "Sure! Shalom. Let me start your release paperwork."

In no time at all, Tanya was back on the street, rolling once again.

CHAPTER ELEVEN

Nothing Is Easy

As Tony sat in the employee's locker room, his coworkers started arriving for the night shift. He needed to finish writing up the maintenance report on the engine before the next shift began, so they'd know where to start their work. But first, he had to clean up any traces of his clothes, blood, and other debris from the engine and hangar floor. He couldn't bring himself to do this without talking to Julie, his bride. *Where did I put my phone?* he wondered. It suddenly dawned on him: He always kept it in his front pocket. Since he was almost shirtless after the engine incident, retrieving it from the hangar became his top priority.

Hurriedly, he grabbed a clean shirt and pair of pants free of blood stains, along with some shoes. As he rushed to dress, he realized Freddie was just around the corner at the next row of lockers. Tony didn't want to talk to him until he had time to gather his thoughts and come up with an explanation. He stopped for a moment to listen for Freddie's exact location so he could quickly escape in the opposite direction. Once he felt sure Freddy was on the far side of the locker room, he swiftly, stealthily, and agilely turned the corner undetected, quietly making his way down the stairs to the hangar floor and the powerful aircraft.

He took his time returning to the turbine engine, opting first to search for his phone on the floor around the massive jet. He had the foresight to bring a trash bag with him to hide any evidence of the accident. In a short time, the bag was full of shoe, pant, and shirt pieces, even some blood and flesh. No wonder Freddie was so upset when he saw the aftermath of it all.

He couldn't locate his phone, so he focused on meticulously removing all traces of evidence from the area. After leaving the trash bag behind, Tony positioned a ladder beneath the silent engine. Armed with cleaning supplies and plenty of rags, he cautiously ascended each rung of the ladder. Considering what had happened last time, his stomach felt a bit queasy.

The blood on the intake cowling and blades immediately drew his attention. It would be impossible to clean up every last drop, out of the question. The plane's maintenance wasn't scheduled for completion for at least three more days. Since he was in charge of the project, he could buy himself some extra time.

He noticed something silver and shiny on the floor near the accident site—his phone. He quickly moved down the ladder, picked it up, and inspected it closely. *Hmm . . . must've fallen out of my pocket.* Surprisingly, it still functioned. He tucked it back into his shirt pocket and continued with the clean-up. Rags piled up at his feet as he worked, and he soon realized the daunting nature of the task. His body may have looked healed, but the trauma from the accident still lingered, making every movement painful and exhausting. He simply wanted to go home, literally and figuratively. In moments like these, he yearned for heaven—to see Jesus again, face-to-face. The longing motivated Tony every day, every year, every millennium as time slowly passed.

Tony's phone vibrated, and Julie's face appeared on the cracked screen. "Hi, babe," he greeted her, a smile forming on his face. "I've been thinking about you."

"Have you now?" Julie responded with her usual kindness and love. "When will you be home?" she asked eagerly.

He hesitated before answering truthfully. "I have a mess at work I need to clean up first," he replied.

"Oh no, what happened?" she asked, concern evident.

He knew the truth wouldn't go over well, but he couldn't bring himself to lie. "An RB211 malfunctioned and caused some damage to the intake blades—"

"Just stop, Tony," Julie interrupted, with disappointment in her voice. "I understand, you'll be working late again." Tony could feel the weight of her words and the hurt behind them.

"You know I love you, right?" he pleaded.

After a brief pause, Julie finally responded with resignation, "Yes dear, goodbye." With a painful shrug of his shoulders, he returned to the task at hand, his heart still yearning for home. After his long day, he finally arrived home, completely drained. He had spent hours cleaning the engine and the surrounding area, making sure to remove any trace of blood. It was just as crucial now as it had been in the past to cover up any evidence. Memories of similar situations flashed through his mind, where concealing the truth had been vital. Truly no one would ever understand except the other two like him.

He cautiously poked his head into the bedroom, making sure not to wake Julie, who was sound asleep. He then made his way to the kitchen and noticed a note on the smooth granite countertop.

Your dinner is in the microwave.
I Love You!

She had surrounded "I Love You" with hearts, her signature touch. Tony smiled and pushed the buttons on the microwave, eagerly anticipating a homemade meal. The accident had taken its toll on him, so this simple act of love from Julie meant a lot.

He looked forward to a hot shower, but he didn't want to disturb Julie so he sneaked into the guest bathroom. The water flowed down and over him, creating a mixture of blood, soap, and water on the shower floor. He scrubbed harder than usual to remove the dried blood out of his scalp and off his body.

As the colorful fluid changed from red to pink, Tony inspected his skin with his hands. His head seemed normal, with no noticeable hair loss. He checked his face next, estimating its condition without the aid of a mirror. Moving on to his chest, it was clear it had taken the brunt of the damage. Chunks of hair were missing; it would take time for them to grow back. Keeping this from Julie would be a challenge. Continuing the examination, he noticed that his legs had suffered major injuries. Though his skin had healed perfectly, patches of missing hair and significant bruising remained. It would take time for those to fully heal too.

As the last droplets of water fell on Tony's head, he froze as he saw Julie standing in the doorway. *Oh my God*, he thought, *she can't see me like this.*

"Hey, honey—" Julie's soft voice rang out from the doorway. Panicked, he grabbed the soap and frantically lathered his body again.

"Hey, babe," he replied with forced nonchalance, trying to regain his composure. "Did I wake you up?"

"No, not really," she responded. "But I'm used to sleeping next to you. When I woke up alone in bed, it startled me. Are you finished? You turned off the shower."

Thinking up a quick excuse, he replied, "I'm taking a 'navy shower.' Trying to conserve water. I'll be out in a minute once I rinse off. I'll see you in the bedroom shortly."

"Okay," Julie said as she turned and left. "You're acting strange today."

Tony let out a sigh of relief as he turned the water back on. It would be a long night ahead and he was exhausted, but he knew he owed Julie an explanation for his odd behavior.

He stepped out of the shower and hastily wiped himself dry, just in case she returned. His thoughts raced as he tried to strategize a plan involving the longest and thickest pajamas he could find. He would need them not just for tonight, but for the next few days as he recovered from his injuries. He made his way down the hallway in his robe, hoping to make it to the bedroom and change into sleepwear without Julie noticing.

As he rummaged through the dresser, Julie lay in bed, pretending to sleep. He finally found the right pajamas and climbed into bed next to her. He could tell she was awake by the way she was breathing. He knew they would end up talking. "What time is it, babe?" he asked, trying to control the conversation about to happen.

"Almost two," Julie replied without moving. "But you know that. Antonio, what is it about you? What am I missing?" Long pause. "Antonio?"

Oh boy, Tony thought, *my full name. Trouble's coming!* He tried to deflect her attention. "I thought that's why you married me," he joked. "It wasn't for my rugged good looks, was it?" Trying to lighten the mood, he continued with a smile. "I actually think you're pretty good-looking." Julie giggled. "Babe, can I pray for us?"

A little surprised, she agreed. "Lord, thank you for my wife Julie. Grant our home perfect peace." And in that very instant, he fell soundly asleep.

CHAPTER TWELVE

Cairoman

Ray had no desire to go to the hospital. He simply longed for a hot shower, to wash away the memories of entrapment and the overpowering scents of death, vermin, and dust. How could Monica snuggle up to him with all that residue on his chest? Evidence of the traumatic event stained his shirt, pants, and socks. Ray dreaded facing the questions that would come with a trip to the hospital. Even someone unfamiliar with forensic evidence could see that something major had occurred to his body.

The ambulance attendant returned to the passenger seat after confirming Ray's vitals were all in order: blood pressure 125/75, respiration at 17 beats per minute; he was dehydrated but otherwise healthy.

"Honey, are you okay?" Monica asked.

"I am now," came the quick reply. Ray released the restraints and managed to sit up on the small gurney, grunting as he did so. He struggled as a tall man to sit up straight in the cramped space of the ambulance. "I'm leaving when we get to the hospital," he declared. "I never wanted to go there in the first place."

"You know they have their protocols, just like everywhere else," Monica reminded him as she scooted back to make room for his large frame.

"Where are you staying?" Ray asked, trying to shift his focus away from the throbbing pain in his head. "I need to clean myself up."

But Monica didn't respond; she was too busy staring at the blood stains on Ray's shirt and pants, the dried blood in his hair from injury. "Ray?" she asked, her voice filled with concern. "Whose blood is that? I don't see any cuts or bruises on you."

Okay, time to put on my acting skills, he thought. He needed a convincing story for Monica and the ambulance attendants, but they wouldn't be the only ones questioning him. "I can't recall everything," he began, knowing it was partially true. "I must have hit my head."

He paused, pretending to think and gather his thoughts. "I vaguely remember hearing someone moaning close by. It could have been a man. I believe I crawled over to where he was . . . Let me try to remember." He stalled for more time. "Yes, now I remember. He was lying on top of some concrete slabs with rebar sticking out of his chest. I think it went through his lungs. There was blood everywhere."

He made his voice tremble as he recounted the events. "There was nothing I could do. He was speaking in Egyptian, and I couldn't understand him. All I could do was hold on to him. I don't know for how long. He died in my arms." He hoped that would suffice as an explanation for the blood on his clothes and his memory loss.

Monica briefly snapped out of her trance over his appearance. "I am so sorry, Ray. I'm relieved that wasn't you. Where were you when the earthquake hit? What were you doing?" Ray's heart raced as he thought about how to answer her questions without uncovering his secret. He buried his head in his hands, pretending to be overcome with emotion.

"I don't know, Monica," he said sternly. "I honestly don't know. I think near the second-floor stairwell." Ray hoped everyone would remember how stairs often remain intact after disasters like this one. "I really don't know," he repeated, lying back on the makeshift bed.

Feeling somewhat satisfied with his explanation, Monica replied, "No need to apologize, Ray."

The Witts finally arrived at their destination; they were oblivious to pulling into the designated spot for emergency vehicles until the attendants opened the back door and unlocked the gurney wheels, preparing to wheel Ray out. Cameras flashed as a media frenzy awaited his arrival. They didn't understand the reporters' words, but they knew what was happening. As a reporter himself, Ray immediately covered his face to avoid being photographed. Monica followed suit, pushing her way through the crowd with her arm up to shield herself. Ray didn't want his picture or face plastered all over the news, but it might be too late for that. He would likely have some explaining to do.

Ray shifted onto his stomach and buried his face in the pillow as the gurney caravan barreled through the emergency entrance of the hospital. The clamor of reporters and people searching for lost loved ones shouting in different languages filled his ears.

"What's happening, Ray? This is beyond normal." Monica's voice cut through the chaos.

"I have no idea. I was underground the past few days!" Ray replied, still reeling from his ordeal.

"You were buried for over five days," Monica replied firmly yet sympathetically.

The paramedics handed Ray over to the doctors and nurses, who quickly led him into a private room. A young doctor, mid-thirties or so, took charge and served up rapid fire orders in Arabic. "هل تتحدث العربية؟؟" [Do you speak Arabic?] he inquired of Ray.

Confused, Ray responded, "What?"

"Oh, you're American," the doctor said, switching to English.

"Yes," Ray confirmed.

The doctor then turned to Monica. "You must leave the room," he instructed her.

Ray immediately protested, sitting up on his new bed. "She's staying with me!" he insisted.

"It's okay, Ray," Monica reassured him as she stepped outside the curtain. "I'll be right outside." As she left, Ray reluctantly settled back onto the bed.

"Good afternoon. I am Dr. Osmon, and I will be conducting your examination today," he declared, taking charge of the situation. "What is your name and how are you feeling?"

"My name is Rayford Witt," came Ray's response. Without looking directly at him, the doctor consulted the charts a nurse handed to him. "I see that your vital signs are all within normal range. Very good," he continued as he picked up his stethoscope. "Take a deep breath and hold it . . . Now exhale . . . Remarkable! Other than some dehydration, you seem to be in perfect condition."

"Great," Ray responded sarcastically. "Can I go now?" he asked impatiently.

"We would like to administer some fluids to rehydrate you, and we recommend a couple days of observation here at the hospital, for further examination."

Ray responded with a firm tone, "If you could prepare my release papers, I'll sign them and relieve the hospital of any liability regarding my condition." Then he added matter-of-factly, "My wife has been waiting anxiously for the past five days, not knowing if I was alive or dead. The best prescription for both of us is to go home."

"As you wish," Dr. Osmon replied, surprising Ray. The doctor left the cubicle to speak with Monica. "Your husband is ready to see you." She ran to Ray's bedside and embraced him tightly. He was relieved that this episode of show and tell was over.

With only one day between his hospital discharge and departure, Ray was already exhausted when he boarded the plane with his wife and colleagues. The flight from Cairo was far from pleasant. He desperately needed rest, while Monica wanted to snuggle. Meanwhile, Steve, Al, and John bombarded him with questions. Mark tried to stay out of the whole situation. Only two hours in, Steve couldn't resist firing off the first one. "Where were you when the earthquake first hit, Ray?" asked Steve. Even though traveling by private jet would save them three hours compared to a commercial flight, it still left plenty of time for annoying inquiries. Ray had planned to use his fatigue, possible memory loss, and trauma as an excuse to avoid difficult discussions.

Ray paused, trying to remember. "I think I had just left my room and gone to the restaurant on the 3rd floor," he replied. He stopped for a moment, adding some dramatic effect. "But then I must have gone to the stairwell. I recall seeing an EXIT sign." Steve leaned in closer, captivated by his account. Al was actually taking notes. "This isn't an official interview, is it Steve?" Ray asked, looking directly at Al. "Oh no," Steve replied with a glare toward Al. Ray wasn't sure if his reaction was due to the notetaking, or Al's lack of discretion.

"After the earthquake, we surveyed your hotel and took some notes and photos," Steve continued. "You were the only survivor inside the building when it collapsed. When the Egyptian and World Press Organization learned of your rescue, there was quite a commotion at the hospital. Do you remember any of that?"

"I definitely remember it, Steve," Ray retorted. "You asked me where I was before the event, and frankly, my memory is hazy after being trapped in that tomb for three days." He chuckled to himself at the irony of his statement.

"Actually, dear, it was closer to five days," Monica reminded him again.

"Oh," Ray replied, holding his head in his hands. "Mark, can I take a look at the photos?"

Mark swiftly reached for the mouse and clicked on a file on his computer screen. He passed the laptop over to Ray, who started examining each slide carefully, making mental notes of every detail. He felt like an attorney examining evidence from the opposing counsel before trial.

He finally found it—the photo he had been searching for—the remains of the stairwell amidst the rubble. Although the building no longer stood, the stairs had remained somewhat intact. Ray managed to force out some tears as he examined the images. He intentionally let his hands tremble and shake, wanting to bring the interrogation to an end. All eyes fixed on his reaction to the photos. Mark stood and took the computer from his lap.

Monica moved to embrace him. "Enough!" she demanded, staring intensely at each man on the plane.

Mark interjected, "Monica, Ray is a skilled journalist and reporter. He's prepared for these types of questions, not just from us at CCJN, but also from the BBC, Reuters, Newsweek, The Post, and many others. Everyone wants to interview 'The Cairoman.'"

"The Cairoman?" Monica asked curiously.

"That's what we're calling Ray now," John added with a smirk. "It's catchy and fitting, isn't it? Egyptian pharaohs, King Tut, tombs . . . It all ties in."

Monica, attentive and caring, looked back at Ray. "Q&A is over! I insist. Let him sleep!"

Ray tried not to let the shock show on his face. As their plane sped through the sky, he had no more need for deception in crying. He couldn't hold back his tears any longer. This could be the beginning of the end. *Maybe it'll all be over soon,* he thought before drifting off into a deep slumber.

As she held on to him, she heard him muttering in his sleep. She leaned closer to make out his words. "God will . . ." he mumbled repeatedly. "God will take care of me."

"One hundred percent true, Ray," Monica whispered as the plane continued its silent journey through the night sky.

The sound of wheels locking in place accompanied the flashing Fasten Your Seatbelt sign. Natasha, the flight attendant, walked through the small cabin to ensure everyone's compliance with the safety protocol. When she reached Ray's seat, Monica subtly gestured for her to move along, whispering, "He's buckled in and fine."

By this point, everyone on the plane realized the extent of Ray's exhaustion. Mark took one look at him and declared, "You need some time off, Ray."

You think? Monica thought sarcastically.

The engines shutting down and doors unlocking were the only reality to reach Ray. None of this felt natural, just supernatural. Despite feeling physically fine, he hardly registered the presence of the reporters that had flooded the small private terminal once they entered it.

Attempting to deal with the media hysteria, Monica instinctively raised her hand and uttered, "No comment," waving Steve over to assist her.

Amidst the chaos of pushing and shoving, a voice rang out. "How did Ray manage to survive under the collapsed building?" Another shouted from the front, "Is it true you had to resort to cannibalism to survive?" This was the last thing he needed.

Mark barked orders to the security team, then asked, "Who leaked information about our arrival?" A young woman shrugged.

As the reporters continued to clamor for his attention, one last voice called out. "Ray, can you give us a statement, as the Cairoman?"

The security officers swiftly turned and guided him out the airport door they had just entered, back onto the tarmac, up the airstairs, and to their seats. Steve barked into his phone, ordering a limousine to come directly to the tarmac, near the plane. "I don't care who said you can't drive a car out here. Make it happen, now!"

Mark leaned over to Al and whispered, "I've never seen Steve act like this. He's completely losing control!"

Al glanced back at Mark. "You better be careful with your words. Ray is well-liked and respected around here. Don't forget where you are." Chastened, Mark quickly took a seat. Minutes later, a large black limousine rolled through the security gate, flashers on. Two armed security police escorted the car to the stairs of the waiting plane.

"Let's move!" Steve exclaimed. The team assisted Ray off the plane and into the waiting limo. The guards slowly guided the vehicle out the gate and safely onto the highway.

"Do we need to take Ray to the hospital, Monica?" Steve asked, his expression filled with concern.

"Absolutely not!" Ray exclaimed firmly. "I have one last stop—my wife, my house, and my bed." Despite Steve's shock at Ray's sudden clarity and determination, he dialed their address on his phone and directed the driver there. As they arrived at the condo, the fog in Ray's mind slowly dissipated, but he knew it would take some time to return to normal. This was perhaps the greatest trauma he had ever experienced; he had no reference point for recovery time. His only constant throughout the ages had been the love of God.

CHAPTER THIRTEEN

Old Friends

Tanya breathed a sigh of relief as she entered the safety of her apartment. Carrie had gone back to work and had classes later that evening. She was happy to have some time to herself. After a long, hot shower, she noticed her clothing scattered on the bathroom floor. They were in shambles—jeans torn, with signs of being dragged on concrete; shirt practically shredded. The evidence clearly pointed to major bodily trauma, although Tanya had none.

She vocalized her thoughts. "There's no way someone wearing those clothes could walk away unscathed." She understood why the doctor and cop had given her such a hard time. And she had a feeling this incident was far from over. After changing into her pajamas, Tanya curled up on the couch and opened the magazine to where she had left off at the restaurant earlier.

She scanned the headlines for the story of the man lost at sea, then took her time reading through the article, making mental notes of every detail. The writing was impressive, but the photography left something to be desired. Apparently, a man named David Long had fallen off a fishing vessel. This went unnoticed for several hours. Finally, the crew realized his absence and searched diligently for him, but could find no trace of him. They presumed him dead, lost at sea, until a passing ship spotted him ten days later clinging to driftwood in the water.

Tanya found it intriguing. How could he have possibly survived so long in those treacherous waters? The average person can only last around three days before succumbing to the dangers of sharks, jellyfish, and freezing temperatures at night. Yet, it seemed this man had defied all the odds. He had utilized his extensive knowledge of survival skills to stay alive. He caught fish, birds, and even turtles for sustenance and cleverly used the turtle's shell to collect rainwater. Mr. Long cited his resourcefulness, adaptability, and unwavering determination as the reasons for his survival.

Tanya pondered, *It could be that, or it could be something else entirely.* She focused on the man's face, hidden behind a thick beard, unkempt hair, and a sunburned complexion with cracked lips. She knew him, despite the changes. She couldn't forget those eyes. Even though she had seen him hundreds of years ago in a different land, his features remained unchanged. His name wasn't David then, and they didn't meet during this time in the Americas. "I have to remember," she determined. Suddenly, she exclaimed, "Lawrence? Larry? No, Leonardo! That's what he called himself." If only she could remember where and when they had crossed paths before.

"God, I could really use your help right now." Tanya prayed, feeling a sense of comfort and reassurance from her faith in Jesus. "I know You're always with me and will continue to be by my side. I feel like it's almost time for me to go home, so please guide me through these difficult waters." As she spoke, a gentle breeze brushed against her face, bringing her peace.

Some papers and pamphlets belonging to Carrie blew off the windowsill and onto the floor. "Great," Tanya grumbled as she got up to retrieve them, but one caught her eye: "Your Next Vacation Destination—Italy!"

"That's it!! I remember. I met him in Italy. Yes, Siena! He took care of the racehorses at Piazza del Campo during the Palio di Siena," she exclaimed excitedly, jumping up and down on the floor and couch. "I can't believe it! That's definitely him!" she declared with uncontrollable joy. She made her way to the kitchen and poured herself a glass of iced tea before settling back onto the couch. "Yes!" Tanya shouted triumphantly. "I've finally found someone who can help me understand who I am!"

CHAPTER FOURTEEN

Enough

Tony's exhaustion weighed heavily on him after a whole night of tossing and turning. As he turned his head to catch a glimpse of sunlight peeking through slightly open blinds, he felt every ache and bruise in his body. *No surprise there,* he sighed. *I'll never make it to work in this state.*

Glancing at the clock, the flashing *10:00 a.m.* stunned him. In a panic, he knocked over the clock while frantically searching for his phone. *Two hours late! Being the boss doesn't excuse me from calling in or showing up.* Finally finding his phone, the bright screen illuminated his face in the dark room. *Why didn't Julie wake me up?* He scanned the room for her, but she was nowhere in sight. Frustrated, he searched through his contacts for his work number.

Julie burst through the door. "Are you okay?" she asked, concerned. "I heard something fall to the ground."

"It was the clock," Tony grumbled. "Why didn't you wake me up? You know I have to be at work by 8 a.m. It's past 10:00!"

"Put down the phone," Julie said calmly. "I called in for you this morning. Phil said you were overdue for a day off." Relieved and slightly embarrassed,

Tony placed his phone on the bedside table and pulled the covers back over himself.

Julie turned on the lights. "Tony, we need to talk," she said with a serious tone.

The dreaded phrase that all men hate to hear, Tony thought silently. "Okay honey," he replied. "Did Phil have anything for me?"

"Yes, he praised your hard work and even called you his favorite employee," she said reassuringly. "You're in the clear, babe. Just get dressed and meet me downstairs for coffee and breakfast." As the door closed behind her, Tony's mind raced: *What did I do? What did I say?* He replayed the last twenty-four hours in his head, trying to figure out the topic for the talk. The thought of getting dressed didn't appeal to him at the moment.

He knew he owed his wife an explanation for his recent strange behavior. She wasn't the first to wonder about it, and she wouldn't be the last. Memories of previous wives who had asked for explanations flooded his mind. Tony remembered Delilah and the incident with the brown bear attack on the Iranian Plateau. He wondered if any of those bears still roamed the area after centuries of human development there. *Beautiful Delilah,* he thought. He never wanted to leave her or the breathtaking Zagros mountain range. Life was simple and idyllic before the attack—growing barley, figs, and tending to livestock for their own use and to sell at the local market. Back then, he went by Amir.

Then, it was easy to be whoever you wanted. But now, with passports, fingerprinting, facial recognition technology—changing identities had become much more complicated. It would have been impossible to explain to Delilah how his savage bear wounds had healed in a matter of days. In this day and age, doctors would have labelled his injuries as massive bodily and facial trauma, with no chance of survival. His only option? Disappear without a trace. And that's exactly what he did—leaving with a healed body but a broken heart, soul, and spirit. Long after he knew Delilah must be dead, he still lamented abandoning her. He would never grow accustomed to outliving everyone he'd ever known and loved. Now, once again, he found himself head over heels in love. This time with Julie, but just the same, he knew he may have to abandon her too.

The sound of the garbage truck rumbling outside snapped Tony out of his thoughts. He needed to head downstairs soon. Procrastinating wouldn't do him any good; it was far too late for that. As he descended the stairs, he could see Julie bustling around in the kitchen, putting away dishes. A plate sat on the counter, already prepared and waiting for him. Tony walked over to the coffeemaker and started brewing his favorite blend. After pouring steaming water into his mug, he pressed the Single Cup button.

"How's your morning so far?" Julie asked with an inquisitive look. "You were tossing and turning all night and talking in your sleep."

"I'm a little tired and achy," Tony replied.

"Achy from what? Can you tell me about it?" Julie pressed for more information. Suddenly, it dawned on him. He had given no thought to how he would explain the mess he had to clean up late last night. "And can you please explain it in simple terms? No complicated jargon this time," Julie asked with a raised eyebrow.

Tony quickly stuffed some food into his mouth, trying to buy himself time to invent a response. "One of the engines had debris caught in it, shredding the blades and causing quite a mess," Tony explained.

Julie wasn't fully convinced and probed further. "What exactly caused the damage?" Tony shifted uncomfortably, quickly stuffing more food in his mouth, then washing it down with coffee. "It was a strange combination of metal, meat, plastic, and other unknown substances," he said nonchalantly, trying to appear unfazed.

"Wow, seriously?" Julie exclaimed. "How did a combination of items like that end up inside a running jet engine?"

"It all happened in an instant," Tony replied. "I was working on the ladder next to the engine when Freddie threw up his metal lunch pail without warning. It contained a variety of things like meat, plastic bags, and a thermos. Unfortunately, I missed it, and the entire pail went straight into the turbine engine. We had to shut everything down. On inspection, we found significant damage. There were bits of debris stuck in the blades. I didn't want to fire Freddie since he's a nice guy, so—"

"Just stop it, Tony!" Julie's irritated voice cut through his words. "I saw your body in the shower last night as I stood in the doorway. I could see the wounds and gaps in your leg and chest hair. So just stop it and tell me the truth. Are you hiding something from me?" she asked again, her tone filled with frustration.

"That is the truth, Julie!" Tony responded, feeling the weight of his lie and praying silently this relationship wouldn't end like the one with Delilah all those years ago. Tony had married Julie for her no-nonsense attitude toward life and her fiery passion. These traits weren't helping at the moment.

"Please come here," he implored, standing and pulling his wife in for a warm embrace. "I love you so much, but there are things I can't tell you right now. I promise I will explain everything soon, but for now, I need you to trust me. Do you trust me, Red? Please, I need you to."

"I love you more than anything, but it's hard for any woman to fully love someone who hides and lies," Julie stated, her voice wavering with emotion. "I'll give you space and time, Tony," she continued, "but I can't wait around forever for you to open up and completely let me in."

In that moment, Tony decided to stop. Stop running and keeping secrets from the woman he loved. He was done sacrificing relationships for secrecy's sake. In every way, he'd had enough.

CHAPTER FIFTEEN

A Secret Place

Tanya needed a break. Her body still ached from the aftermath of the accident and the rough landing that followed. Although she had superficially healed, she couldn't shake off the soreness that came with such an intense collision. She decided to take some vacation time from work.

She sat alone in the house with a cup of black coffee in hand; Carrie had already left for work. She settled into a comfy chair to check her social media accounts, starting with her favorite, TikTok. Then, scrolling through Twitter, Facebook, and Instagram, she sarcastically commented on what was happening in her world. She rolled her eyes at all the mindless chatter and mundane posts on her feed. It all seemed so trivial. *Who really cares about someone's favorite restaurant or recipe? And no one wants to see a picture of your main dish either,* she thought. After cleaning out her inbox, full of junk emails, she moved on to responding to friends.

Feeling drowsy, she took another sip of coffee, hoping to wake up. The jolting knock on the door did the trick. *Who could that be? Only Carrie knows I'm home,* Tanya wondered as she made her way to the door. Peering through the peephole, Dr. Abrams from the ER surprised her, standing outside.

What in the world? Tanya gasped, unsure what to do. She could simply ignore the knock, but something inside her urged her: *Open the door!* Tanya recognized that voice—the one in her soul where she felt connected to God and received guidance, not in a religious, but in a relational way. This connection had been constant throughout her entire life; God's presence went deeper than the illusory "voice in your head."

As the door opened, the doctor extended her hand. "It's a pleasure seeing you again, Tanya. Do you remember me? I'm Dr. Abrams from Mercy Hospital."

"Yes, of course, doctor. I remember you," Tanya replied. "I'm just surprised by the house call," she added, interested yet guarded.

The doctor paused in front of her doorway. "May I enter?" she asked politely.

Tanya nodded and stepped aside to let her in. "Sure, come in." Tanya gestured toward an empty chair at the kitchen table.

"Let me get straight to the point," Dr. Abrams offered, and Tanya appreciated her directness. She navigated life the same way.

"I pulled your address from your file, something I've never done before and don't plan to do again," the doctor confessed with concern in her voice. "I hope you won't report me to my superiors, but you are a very special case."

"Go on," Tanya urged her.

"Like you, I am also Jewish—a Messianic Jew, to be exact. Are you familiar with Jews who believe in Jesus?"

"Sure." She purposely kept her response short, her curiosity growing.

"My family has a rich ancestral history that dates back before the common era. We came originally from the tribe of Levi, and later became known as the Essenes. Our most famous association is with the Dead Sea Scrolls found in Qumran.

"Even John the Baptist was an Essene, right doctor?" Tanya asked, already knowing the answer.

"Yes," Dr. Abrams replied. "Shall I continue?"

"Yes, please do," Tanya eagerly answered.

"Most people, whether Jewish or not, are unaware that we still exist today. We have always been present but have remained hidden within the confines of Judaism. I won't bore you with all the details of our history, but the Essenes have always been guardians of Judaism's dark secrets."

"So, you're saying your community is still alive and well? That can't be true, doctor. Everyone knows the Essenes died out after Josephus. During the diaspora, they scattered everywhere." Tanya wasn't just reciting history; she knew this firsthand. She had been there through it all. "The first Roman revolt in the first century practically destroyed them, and you're telling me you're still around today? I find that hard to believe."

"Tanya, it's not only possible, it's true. We are still here and thriving, mainly because of you."

"What?" Tanya exclaimed, jumping out of her seat. "Because of me?"

"Yes," the doctor confirmed.

"I know who you are. I knew it from your initial exam, and it became even more apparent in your eagerness to leave. The officer on scene was convinced you shouldn't have survived the collision with that truck. And I wouldn't be surprised if the police investigate further." She continued firmly and full of confidence, "In my opinion, your best course of action is to let me assist you."

"Dr. Abrams, you need to leave," Tanya said firmly, gesturing toward the door.

The doctor stood purposefully. "Tanya, I am here to make sense of everything for you. I know the reason you insisted on keeping that magazine," she said, pointing at the coffee table. "You and the others like you are not alone. It's time to put an end to all of this and help you all go home. God's Word is very clear: Our ways and God's are not the same. He moves not only in mysterious ways but in mysterious times and seasons. Now is your time, your season." With those words, she turned, walked down the hallway, and disappeared.

CHAPTER SIXTEEN

Truth and Consequences

The article on Tanya's accident didn't make the front page of the newspaper. It was relegated to the third page, where mundane and ordinary events were typically reported. But the simple title, "Local Woman Hit by Truck," caught Tony's attention. He was no stranger to reading such articles and quickly retrieved his scissors to carefully cut it out. Adding it to his collection of similar stories, he committed the relevant information to memory: street name, truck driver's information, witnesses, etc. It had been a few days since Tony and Julie had talked, and he was relieved she had backed off for now.

Julie laughed with her best friend Kay in the living room. Tony could slip away for a few hours unnoticed. He made a quick stop in the kitchen before leaving. "Hey, honey, I'm stepping out for a bit," he announced as he grabbed a bottle of water and bag of chips.

"What?" Julie yelled from the living room.

Tony walked to her there, snacking on chips. "I'm going to the city for a bit."

"Oh really?" Kay interjected. "I was just there a few days ago. What's your plan?"

"Yeah, what's going on, Tony?" Julie asked with a sly smile.

"I just want to take a ride on the trains and get some fresh air," he replied smoothly.

"You gonna meet up with Chris?" Kay asked, thinking of her husband.

"I'd like some alone time," Tony stated firmly.

"Yeah, sometimes he just needs to be by himself. It's a shared trait between us," Julie confirmed.

"That's why I adore this woman," Tony exclaimed, grinning at Julie. "She keeps life interesting. Now kiss me you fool," Tony joked as he lifted Julie up and spun her around and into a dip.

"What a hopeless romantic," Kay remarked as he headed toward the door.

"You know it!" he replied with a wink and a tip of his baseball cap to the ladies.

Tony took a short stroll to reach the New Jersey Northeast Corridor Transit Station. He boarded the Northbound train with ease, knowing it would take him straight to Manhattan, crossing through New Jersey and over the Hudson River. The 45-minute ride always filled up with interesting characters: dancers, youngsters blasting music, beggars, and pickpockets. As the train came to a halt at Penn Station, he stood, ready to exit. A woman carrying a baby on her back approached him. "Excuse me sir, do you have any spare change? My baby is hungry."

Tony had heard that phrase countless times before. Without a second thought, he reached into his pocket and pulled out a $20 bill for her. Her face lit up with gratitude as she jokingly reminded him, "You know I can't make change, right?"

"Of course," Tony replied with a smile.

"God bless you, sir," the woman said as she made her way up the stairs.

Exactly, Tony thought. He was no stranger to the scriptures about helping the poor or showing kindness to strangers. They could be angels in disguise. His favorite Bible quote had remained constant over the ages: "It is better to give than receive."[3]

After arriving at the Manhattan Transfer Station, he quickly boarded the Green Line and rode it to his destination at 96th Street, the nearest stop to the accident. As he emerged from the underground subway system, he couldn't help but admire the towering skyscrapers dominating the southern horizon. Fantastic! He had seen many impressive structures in his lifetime— medieval castles, the Pyramids of Giza, Petra of Jordan—but none compared to the grandeur of these modern buildings.

His mind drifted back to memories of the Colosseum in Rome, a place with special significance for Tony (then known as Baruch). Many of his friends had tragically lost their lives there. Their names and faces flashed through his mind: Eli, the one exalted; Eitan, his strong and loyal friend; Reuven, the warrior; Shimon, always heard by God; and Uri, who found good in everyone, a beacon of light even in the darkest moments. He hoped

---

[3] Acts 20:35, author paraphrase

that New York City—the Big Apple—would be his last stop on his long and epic journey.

He reached the intersection of Madison Avenue and 103rd Street without any complications, then immediately recognized the Greek café mentioned in the article, along with Petrocelli's, a street market on the corner. This spot marked the exact location of the accident. Tony crossed the street to ask the workers at Petrocelli's if they had seen or heard anything related to it.

He approached a man in an apron, washing fruits and vegetables with a hose. "Good morning, sir," he greeted him.

"Good-a morning to you," came the reply from Morty, the old man's strong Italian/New York accent singing out. "You wanna some fruit, or somethin' else?" he asked.

"No, thank you," Tony declined. "I was wondering if you saw the accident here involving a young woman? I believe it happened about a week ago."

"Did-a I see the accident? Did-a I see the accident? I was a-standing right-a here when that nice-a girl gotta hit by that truck. You should-a seen her flyin' through-a the air. Mama Mia! It was-a terrible!" Morty exclaimed, flailing his arms and splashing water around the sidewalk.

"How far did she fly?" Tony asked.

"Oh, she flew-a like a bird and hit-a the ground right-a there in front-a me," he said, pointing to the spot. "I just-a know she's-a dead." He made the sign of the cross: head, heart, chest. Tony had no problem getting any information from him.

"Hey, you a reporta or sumpthin'?" inquired Morty.

"No, sir," Tony replied. "I read about it in the paper and wanted to speak with the hero who helped that woman."

"Hero?" the man questioned, confused.

"Yes, you were the first one to help her, weren't you?" Tony confirmed.

"Wella, I never thought of-a myself as a hero" the man said, blushing a little. "I just-a did what-a anybody would do."

A petite elderly woman, Beatrice, interrupted the conversation. "That's-a right, he is-a no hero, it was I who-a first reached-a that poor girl," she announced as she pushed in front of her husband. "She was-a knocked silly and-a bleeding from-a her head, legs, and-a shoulders. What a mess!"

"Was she unconscious?" Tony inquired.

"No," they both replied in unison. "Keep-a quiet, old man," Beatrice scolded her husband, "you-a only know what-a I told you."

"And where did they take her?" Tony pressed.

"To-a Mercy Hospital," they answered together once more. "That-a girl in the café told-a me, not-a you," she corrected Morty again. The old man grumbled and returned to watering the plants.

"Are-a you married?" Beatrice suddenly interjected.

"What?" The question caught Tony off guard.

"Are-a you married?" she repeated.

"Yes," Tony confirmed.

"Too-a bad," the old woman remarked with a sigh, "you and-a that girl-a would-a make a nice couple." With that, she turned and disappeared into the market.

Tony seized his chance to leave before Morty started talking again, and made his way to the little café on the corner. *Now we're getting somewhere!*

The quaint little café appealed to Tony. The attention to old Greek decorum impressed him. The bell over the door signaled his arrival, and the hostess came to the door with a menu. "How many in your party?"

"Just me," Tony replied.

"Will the bar be alright, sir?" she inquired.

"I would prefer a booth, please," Tony stated as they walked to the table. His waitress soon arrived. "Hello, I'm Carrie and I'll be your server today. Can I bring you another drink?"

"No, water is fine," Tony said. "Finest in the country," he added with a grin as he took a sip. "Or at least that's what they tell me about New York water."

"Are you ready to order?" asked Carrie, polite, yet ignoring the banter.

"I believe so. I'll have the special."

"Would you like fries or chips with that?" inquired Carrie.

"Fries, please."

"Alright, I'll put that order in for you," Carrie assured him before walking away.

Tony turned to observe the small café more closely from his booth. *Could anyone inside have seen the accident happen?* He took out the newspaper clipping, noting the woman hit by the truck had left this café just before it occurred. *Someone in here must have witnessed it.*

Carrie cleaned the table next to him with a large, damp rag. *She seems friendly enough*, Tony thought. "Excuse me, do you have a moment?"

"Sure," Carrie replied. "How can I help you?"

"Were you working here a few weeks ago when that woman got hit by a truck on this corner?" Tony asked, pointing outside.

Carrie's demeanor shifted immediately. "Are you a cop or another reporter?" she inquired, adding with frustration, "Everyone's looking for a story."

"Oh, no," Tony said reassuringly. "I'm not a reporter. I'm a friend of Mr. and Mrs. Petrocelli," he explained, gesturing toward the market.

"Who isn't?" Carrie retorted.

"Well, they are quite the pair," Tony agreed with a chuckle, trying to ease the tension. "Mrs. Petrocelli sure keeps him in check," he joked.

"She certainly does," Carrie acknowledged. "How do you know them? I've never seen you around here before."

"That's true. I just came in from Jersey," Tony said, blending truth with fiction. "Anyway, about the accident—what happened, Carrie?" he asked, noting her name tag.

"I not only saw it—my roommate was the woman hit," Carrie said, finishing up the table. "It was super scary at the time, but she's fine now. Good as new," she added before walking away. That was all Tony needed to hear.

The meal was pleasant, and during the course of it, Tony learned from Carrie that her roommate worked for the city, frequently visited this café for lunch, and lived within walking distance of it. As he headed back to the subway, he felt a deep sense of breakthrough in his soul. His journey had been long and arduous, but now his mind, body, and spirit yearned for closure. Could this mysterious woman be the key, the answer his soul had been searching for? A clue to the way home? A voice inside him whispered, *Yes*.

Tony returned to his apartment to find Kay gone. Julie was bustling around, tidying up from her lunch with Kay. He stepped into the kitchen and Julie asked, "How was your trip to the city? Did you find what you were looking for?"

"What do you mean?" Tony replied.

Julie picked up a newspaper and flipped to the page where Tony had carefully cut out an article.

Oh, man. His body language gave him away.

"Is this why you went into town?" Julie asked, tracing her finger around the hole where the article used to be.

"Yes," Tony admitted.

"Do you want to tell me about it?" Julie pressed. "But before you start, I have to tell you—I went online and found the story you cut out. I read it. So instead of playing games, just tell me the truth."

He needed a moment to compose himself. "Can't I come in and just relax for a bit? The train ride was rough, and I could use a breather."

Julie responded with a warm smile. "Of course. Take your time. Just make sure you're back here in ten minutes," she replied, motioning to the living room couch.

Tony retreated to the bedroom, kicked off his shoes, changed his clothes, and took a few moments to gather his thoughts. Maybe telling the truth would be best after all.

He appeared from the bedroom to find Julie on the couch, arms and legs crossed, waiting for him.

He attempted to break the tension. "How did your visit with Kay go?"

"Fine," Julie replied in a curt tone, a hint of anger and confusion in her voice.

"Is there something wrong? Are you upset with me?"

"Well, let's see," Julie began, her tone growing more heated. "You lied about how you got hurt, lied about how quickly you healed, and then lied about going to the city for fresh air when really it was to see another woman. So yes, Tony, I may be a little angry. And hurt. And frustrated!" she finished painfully.

Tony shifted uncomfortably on the couch, acknowledging the truth of everything she said. "It's not what you think, Julie," he tried to explain.

"Oh? Then what is it?" she inquired, her tone a little more forceful.

"Julie, you know I have no family. I don't even know who my parents are, or if I have any siblings. I'm completely alone," Tony said. Her expression softened from anger to hurt. He quickly added, "I have you and your family—that means everything to me. But I still feel like I have no one of my own."

Julie pulled out her iPad and began reading the missing article: "A delivery truck hit a pedestrian after the young woman unexpectedly stepped off the curb into oncoming traffic. The incident occurred at 12:47 p.m. on Thursday near the intersection of Madison Avenue and 103rd Street. Witnesses reported the impact threw her approximately thirty feet onto the curb, yet she sustained no major injuries. Do you know her, Tony? They didn't mention her name, but the address was . . . Is that where you went?"

"Yes," he confirmed.

"Why?" Julie inquired out of curiosity.

"I wanted to see for myself how she managed to survive such a severe injury and still remain conscious," explained Tony.

"That doesn't make any sense."

"I know," Tony sighed as he stood up. "Hold on. I want to show you something."

He headed to the garage, grabbed a ladder, and retrieved a box from the top shelf. He emptied its contents onto his workbench and searched for two large manila envelopes. Once he found them he brought them inside, then emptied them onto the coffee table.

Julie reviewed them one by one, each a news article. "'Man Returns Home Following Avalanche'; 'Plane Crashes in the Andes, Lone Survivor'; 'Police Officer Survives Shot to the Chest'; 'Woman Lives Through Horrific Boating Accident.' Tony, there must be at least twenty-five articles here. What is this?" she asked.

"More like forty," he corrected her.

"I don't understand," she said, confused by the collection.

"You opened this box," Tony said as he leaned in closer to her. "The truth is, I'm searching for others like me."

"You mean other Jewish people?" she asked, her curiosity piqued.

"Yes, but something more as well," he clarified.

"More?" Her confusion increased.

"I believe there may be someone out there who possesses the same rapid healing abilities that I have. Someone with similar DNA."

"Like a sibling or relative?" Julie asked, trying to make sense of it all.

"Yes, something like that," Tony said, partly looking for an escape and partly telling the truth, torn between a desire to reveal everything and maintain some secrets. "I have a feeling someone out there is like me, and that we may be related. It's a longshot, but I'm hoping to find them," he admitted.

"So, you're looking for survivors of accidents?"

"It may not make sense, but this need to belong and understand myself consumes me." Tony's words poured out as he opened his heart. "Will you help me with this? I need your support now more than ever. My body may heal quickly, but my soul is aching, deeply," he cried out in desperation.

"I'll do whatever I can," she promised, love clear in her words. "Right now, I won't ask any questions. Just don't push me away and don't lie to me. Promise me that and we can work through this together."

"I promise," Tony replied. "Let's start right now. I don't know the woman in that accident, but something compelled me to talk to her. So, I went to the location of the incident and spoke to witnesses. No one understands her extreme recovery. I want to meet her and hear her side of the story."

"How do you plan on accomplishing that?" Julie inquired.

"I'm not entirely sure," he admitted. "Apparently she came out of a nearby café just before the accident. I talked to a waitress there, her roommate. I figure I'll start there and see if she returns to the area. If she does, I'll try to talk to her."

"Great!" Julie exclaimed, catching Tony off guard with her support. "What can I do to help?"

"Let me think about it," he replied with immense gratitude. For the first time in his long life, he had a genuine ally, one he wouldn't lose.

.

CHAPTER SEVENTEEN

Dreams

Ray was gradually starting to feel like his old self again. The reporters, cameras, and curious onlookers became a rare sight each day, although a handful of persistent snoops still lurked around. *I can't stay cooped up in the condo forever. The question is, When do I make my escape?*

Monica had been a blessing, managing all the incoming calls and dealing with the occasional bold reporter who showed up at their door. On a positive note, all the unwanted attention had tripled Monica's genealogy and research business since Ray returned home. However, sifting through the barrage of nonsense calls, emails, and social media messages proved to be daunting for her.

Ray poured himself a cup of coffee and sat down in the living room; Monica joined him on the couch. "How are you feeling today, babe?" she asked.

"I'm good," he replied. "Why do you ask?"

"The past few nights, you've been talking in your sleep."

"What did I say? Was it important?"

"I'm not sure," Monica said. "Your voice was calm and clear, but the words didn't make any sense. You were speaking in foreign languages."

"What?" he exclaimed. "A foreign language?"

"Not just one," Monica clarified, "multiple foreign languages."

Ray knew he should feign surprise, but with his fluency in at least seven languages, it was difficult to truly seem shocked. Moving from country to country and immersing himself in various cultures had made language acquisition almost effortless for him. Spending centuries in Europe had secured his fluency in the romance languages, while Hebrew remained his primary language, followed by Greek and the Persian languages, including Farsi. *What did she hear me say?*

"Ray," she said, snapping him out of his reverie. "You spoke for so long that I recorded you."

"Seriously, Monica?" he replied, slightly annoyed. Then, he blurted out, "Why would you do that?"

"You scared me, Ray!" she sighed, pulling out her phone. "You know my job requires me to interact with all sorts of people and languages, so it's not just the foreign languages that bother me, but something more profound. Just listen to it, please?" Hearing the pain in her voice, he reluctantly agreed.

התיבה יתוא איבת השקבב אבא התיבה רוזחל הצור ינא
[I want to come home. Father, please bring me home.]

ילש תבלו יתשאל התיבה תכלל הצור ינא אבא אבא
[Abba Father, I want to go home to see my wife and daughter.]

Ray heard himself, desperately pleading in Hebrew for release and reunion with his family. The intense emotion nearly brought him to tears as he listened. No wonder it upset Monica. Despair is universal.

She paused the recording and turned to Ray with a worried expression. "What does all of this mean? Why were you sobbing?"

If I tell her the truth, she'll know I speak Hebrew. She'll know I long to be free and return home, he thought. The door to his past would open wide, exposing his secrets and the truth. *If I don't respond, she'll find someone to translate the recording. She's not a child—I can't take her phone away.* He decided to move forward. "Anything else?" he inquired.

"Yes, there's more," Monica replied with disappointment as she played another recording. He repeated the same phrases. "I want to be free. *I want to go home,*" this time in a flawless Persian dialect.

"Is that all?"

"No," Monica muttered as she began the next recording. This time, he repeated the same phrase in clear, concise Arabic.

"Well?" Monica questioned.

"I'm not sure what to say, Moni," Ray replied, furrowing his brow. "You know I travel all over the world, so I've picked up bits and pieces of different languages."

"Ray!" Monica's voice boomed, "What did you say and what does it mean?"

"I don't know, babe," Ray snapped, "just gibberish, I suppose."

But then, clear as a bell, she played a recording in English. "I want to be free; I want to go home." Over and over again, he passionately pleaded for his homecoming.

Tears streaming down her face, Monica looked into Ray's eyes. "Do you love me?"

"With all my heart," he assured her emphatically.

"Then it's time to tell me the truth. The whole truth!" she insisted, emotionally.

"Darling, I love you completely, and there's no one else for me," Ray cried. "Being with you is where I belong," he continued, his nightly dreams about to invade his reality. For both his sake and hers, he knew this couldn't continue long.

"Then why were you longing for freedom, for going home?" Monica asked desperately. "Is that what you were saying in all those languages? How do you even know that many dialects? And don't give me that 'from your job' nonsense. That's a lie, Ray!"

The doorbell rang, breaking the tension. Ray let out a sigh of relief and headed toward the sound. He opened the door to find a boy, about thirteen or so, standing there with boxes of candy in his hands. "Excuse me sir, can you help us with our church fundraiser? We're trying to raise enough money to send our youth group to the Holy Land."

Ray was still focused on his conversation with Monica. "Can you help us?" the boy repeated.

Ray reached in his pocket for his wallet, then realized it was upstairs on the dresser. "Monica, do you have $10 for this kid?" he asked. She already had her hand in her purse. "All I have is $20," she said, placing the money into Ray's hand.

The boy took hold of their hands. "God bless you both!"

As three hands touched, something shifted. All the tension and angst vanished.

"Thank you! Have a blessed and beautiful day," the boy said cheerfully as he descended the porch stairs and left.

They stood still for a moment, looking at their intertwined hands. Some power had unified them again.

"Monica, there's something important I need you to do," Ray said calmly as he closed the door.

"What is it?" she murmured.

"I want you to use your expertise as a professional genealogist to dig up all the information you can find on me."

"What do you mean?" she asked, intrigued.

"No one is better than you at tracing someone's history. You know I am Jewish, but nothing beyond that," he replied.

"Well, that's because you told me you have no living family—no brothers, no sisters, no aunts or uncles, no one."

"Everyone has someone," Ray countered. "Isn't that the motto on all your letterhead?"

"Absolutely! Everyone does have someone if you search hard enough," Monica affirmed confidently.

"Then, I'm at your disposal," he assured her. "Once you've completed your research, if you find someone related to me, I'll explain everything to you."

"Deal!" Monica declared loudly. *Ray's very clever, and he knows I won't back down from this challenge; it's not in my nature. What he doesn't know is that I'll devote every waking moment to uncovering the truth,* she resolved. *I'll use every resource available to get to the bottom of his story.*

"Come here, my love," he said softly, and gathered her into his arms.

CHAPTER EIGHTEEN

Judah

Dr. Abrams' visit perplexed Tanya. It seemed impossible that anything the doctor had said could be true, yet she spoke with such conviction. Tanya heard a familiar voice again: *Truth is truth, and the truth shall set you free.* The voice mixed with the echo of the doctor's words.

Visibly shaken, Tanya rose from the couch and walked over to her computer. With determined fingers, she typed in "Dr. Abrams, Mercy Hospital," and several names appeared on-screen. The first two were male doctors, so she clicked on the third option. It brought up a picture of the good doctor. "Alexandra Abrams, MD," she read aloud, smirking. *She thinks she knows so much about me; it's time I learn a little about her.*

Alexandra Abrams MD, Mercy Hospital, New York, NY

Board Certifications—American Board of Surgery, 2004; General Surgery, 2005

Medical Education—Tel-Aviv University, MD, 1989

Tanya paused, considering the information. In addition to Dr. Abrams' extensive medical education and experience, she had also taken numerous trips dedicating her services to Doctors Without Borders, an international humanitarian organization. Tanya also learned she was fifty-seven, married, and genuinely Jewish, giving her a glimpse of the person behind the white coat. With determination, Tanya quickly dressed and ordered an Uber to 15431 West 192nd Avenue, Manhattan, giving her about ten minutes to get down to the street.

The ride to the hospital was as chaotic and bustling as any typical New York experience, with traffic, honking horns, and people crowding the sidewalks. *Just the way I like it*, Tanya thought. When she arrived at the hospital, she instructed the driver to drop her off at the emergency room entrance.

"Is everything alright? Is this an emergency?" Roger, the driver, asked her.

"No, I'm just meeting a doctor friend of mine," she replied, thanking him and paying him for the ride.

She boldly walked up to the reception area, overflowing with sick patients. Some coughed uncontrollably, while others moaned in pain while holding blood-soaked clothes over their injuries. She got into line, wishing she had brought a mask. Far too many people were rocking back-and-forth, talking to themselves, for Tanya's comfort. As she waited in the slow-moving line, time passed at a snail's pace. She began drowning in the waves of despair and hopelessness, unsure what she would even say once she reached the front of the line.

A constant stream of medical professionals were entering and exiting a nearby door. *I might as well give them a try.* She made her way toward an area near the door and waited for someone who looked approachable to walk by. She spotted a young man heading her way; he noticed her before she even saw him.

Yes! Tanya's mind raced. *He sees me, and he looks interested.*

"Can I be of assistance?" the young doctor asked.

"I don't know," Tanya responded, trying to sound as despondent as possible.

"Are you feeling unwell?" Dr. Samuelson asked, his name tag catching her eye.

"No. I'm actually looking for my aunt. We were supposed to meet here in the ER, but I can't seem to find her."

"What's her name?" the doctor inquired.

"Dr. Abrams," Tanya said.

"Oh, she's one of my supervising doctors. I'm a resident here at Mercy," Dr. Samuelson explained.

"Oh, really?" She tried to sound interested.

"Yes, but she doesn't start her shift for another six hours, at 7:00 tonight."

"What?" Tanya acted surprised. "I must have gotten my days and times mixed up," she quickly lied.

"Yes. We all work twelve-hour shifts, so it's easy to get confused," the naive doctor shared.

"Where are you from, doc?" Tanya asked, trying to divert the conversation.

"A little town called Norwich, New York. Have you heard of it?"

"No," she replied, ready to leave.

"Well, maybe I can show it to you sometime?" Dr. Samuelson suggested flirtatiously.

"Maybe," Tanya replied as she turned to walk away.

"Can I have your number?" the young doctor asked eagerly.

"I'll have to ask my aunt first," Tanya said, backing the young doctor down.

"Oh, of course," he stammered, then disappeared through the door.

Now it's my turn, Tanya thought as she blended back into the bustling city streets. *I'll do a little recon of my own!*

For Tanya, rising early was nothing out of the ordinary. Working for the city meant she usually left home by 5:00 a.m. each day, so she and RJ could start their route on time. Today, her mission was to gather as much information about Dr. Abrams as possible. The subway would take her to the hospital directly: Red line to blue line, just a few stops and she'd be there.

The journey was uneventful, and Tanya emerged from the stairs near the hospital. Logic suggested Dr. Abrams would leave the facility near the ER lobby, so Tanya positioned herself strategically in that area. Armed with a cup of coffee and a muffin, she had a clear view of at least three hospital exits.

Relentless sounds of sirens and flashing lights filled the parking area, like a conveyor belt of white, red, and blue vehicles arriving and departing. Tanya glanced at her watch: 6:45 a.m., time for a shift change. Streams of personnel in white and blue dress entered the building, giving Tanya an awe-inspiring view: so many people coming together to help others, to save lives.

Gradually, the exchange of workers unfolded as the tired staff finishing their shifts left the hospital. Tanya stayed alert, observing every person exiting. Tall ones, short ones, some exhausted, others laughing and talking, and some departing silently, all heading home.

By 7:15, fifteen minutes past Dr. Abrams' scheduled shift end, Tanya realized the doctor may not have come to work that day. Yet within minutes Tanya saw her, head down, walking briskly, finally emerging from the building and moving right toward her. Tanya quickly, skillfully slipped into a nearby doorway. The doctor passed by in mere seconds, completely unaware of her.

As they descended the subway stairs and moved through the turnstile, Tanya followed Dr. Abrams onto a train car. As the doors closed, Tanya turned her back to the doctor. *I'm a spy on a mission.* At least ten to fifteen people sat between them, giving her space to discreetly observe Dr. Abrams' actions. She glanced back at each stop to check on the doctor before continuing their journey.

Tanya noticed the diverse group of people on the train, though New Yorkers customarily made no eye contact. She could easily identify hospital workers;

they carried themselves with a certain air and many still wore their work attire. As the train reached the Elmhurst exit, the doctor got off and so did Tanya, maintaining a safe distance. They went up the stairs and through the tunnel, Dr. Abrams walking quickly and purposefully. Tanya kept pace with her from across the street.

As they turned the corner, multiple people greeted Dr. Abrams with nods, obviously a familiar face in this neighborhood. Outside Café Roma, a man around her age welcomed her with a kiss. *Ahh . . . her husband,* Tanya concluded anxiously. *Great. What am I gonna to do now? None of the shops are open at this hour. I stick out like a sore thumb.* Lost in thought, she didn't notice a man approaching.

"Are you Tanya Bloom?" he inquired.

Wow. I'm really not cut out for detective work. "Yes, sir," she replied, barely managing the words.

"I'm Benjamin Abrams. Would you like to join my wife, Alexandra, and me for coffee? We'd love to chat with you now that you're here."

I've been made. Guess I'll just make the most of it. "Sure, I'd love to," she replied. *Who's tracking who? Am I the hunter or the hunted?*

As Tanya walked alongside Mr. Abrams, she couldn't help but feel a mix of embarrassment and frustration for getting caught. He broke the tense silence by motioning toward their booth in the back of the café, where they could "have some privacy."

Benjamin spoke in a strong Middle Eastern accent, reminding Tanya of the many years she had lived in Israel, immersed in that culture. From his movements, attire, and overall demeanor, he was likely a highly religious Jewish man, possibly even a member of the clergy, such as a rabbi, Kohen, Levite, or Rebbe.[4] *I suppose I'll find out the truth soon enough,* she thought. Benjamin took his seat next to his wife, and Tanya sat across from them in the booth.

"Hello, Tanya." Alexandra greeted her, with a surprisingly gentle voice, a stark contrast to the matter-of-fact, almost pushy demeanor she had displayed at Tanya's apartment and the hospital. "I'm glad you're here," she said warmly. "We have been awaiting your arrival for a very, very long time."

"Aren't you curious as to why I followed you?" Tanya asked.

"On the contrary," she responded calmly. "The Essenes have been waiting for you for ages, even for centuries or a millennium. Not just my husband and I, but our entire group. In fact, my husband and I have spent our lives searching for you," she added. "Do you remember what we discussed in your apartment?"

Tanya paused, considering her question carefully before responding. "This is so much to take in. I remember telling you that the Essenes died out centuries ago."

Benjamin leaned forward, sensing her hesitation. "How do you personally feel about what we're asserting? What did you learn in the past?"

[4] A rabbi is a teacher/judge on matters of religious law; Kohens are descendants of Moses' brother Aaron, the original High Priest, and a subset of the Levite tribe; a Levite is a descendant of Levi, the third son of Jacob, whose primary call was to serve God in temple duties, including sacrifices and worship; and Rebbes are leaders of the Hasidic community of Jews.

Tanya took a deep breath before answering. "Honestly, I feel conflicted. It's hard to reconcile what you're saying with what I've always believed."

Alexandra nodded in agreement. "Your thoughts are partially correct, but our identity has always been clear to us. In the tenth century, God gave us (the Essenes) a mission when we settled in London, York, Oxford, and Bristol, after leaving Normandy due to the Norman conquest of England. During this time, God spoke to Judah Halevi, a renowned poet, philosopher, and scientist.

"Do you know him, Tanya?" Benjamin asked.

"Do you mean do I have knowledge about him?" Tanya clarified, her countenance changing.

"No!" he exclaimed with certainty. "I'm asking if you personally knew him."

Tanya's eyes welled up with tears, reminiscing over her memories of Spain. She knew Judah; she was his wife. The memories flooded back, and tears streamed down her cheeks. She loved him and their daughter, Abigail, more than life itself. Judah was not just a poet, but a passionate lover who brought all his talents and devotion to God into their marriage. Tanya wept openly, remembering their relationship. Long ages had passed since she had allowed herself to think about him and Abigail.

Benjamin stood and Alexandra moved next to Tanya, wrapping her arms around her and holding her silently in her distress, offering comfort without words.

"I had to leave them behind, but I loved them so much," she cried.

"I understand, dear," Alexandra replied reassuringly. "You needed to protect your identity."

"How do you know all of this?" Tanya asked, composing herself.

"Our group discovered Judah's writings about your departure after he passed away," the doctor explained. "He left them for our community, the Essenes. And your name, Halevi, is a reminder of his identity as a Levite."

"The writing revealed that as time passed and Judah aged, you did not. You and your daughter appeared as the same age when you left, right?" Benjamin inquired.

"Do you want me to confirm that?" Tanya asked dryly.

"Yes, Athalia," he replied with a knowing smile.

Tanya's face lit in recognition of her former name. "My husband had just finished writing his most famous work, The Kuzari, when the First Crusade erupted. It seemed the perfect time to leave," she replied. "Leaving Cordoba was the second most traumatic event in my life, at least up to that point. There were too many questions I didn't want to answer or explain. Too many! I had promised myself I would never marry or have children. I broke that promise and a lot of people suffered: Judah, Abigail, and her husband, Abraham, to mention a few."

"And you too," Alexandra added.

"Yes, I suppose me too," Tanya said, eyes tearing up again.

"Would you like to see what Judah wrote?" Benjamin asked.

"You have something he wrote?" Her curiosity piqued as she came back to life.

"Yes, we do," he affirmed.

"Yes, yes, I want to see it. When? where?"

"Well, right now if you want. It is in our apartment," he offered. Tanya stood and headed for the door as the elderly couple gave chase.

Their modest and unassuming apartment surprised Tanya; she didn't expect it on a doctor's income. Jewish and Christian cultures blended throughout the space, coexisting in harmony. On the mantle sat a Star of David next to an ivory carving of Jesus and the Last Supper. A menorah adorned the dining room table, while a depiction of Jesus hung on the wall in the center of the room, accentuating it. In the living room, Tanya picked up a shofar from the coffee table. "Can you play this?" she asked Benjamin.

"Yes, we both know how to play it. We usually reserve it for special occasions."

Alexandra chimed in. "I think this is a special occasion, Benjamin."

"I couldn't agree more," he said as he retrieved the shofar from its holder and carefully wiped it down with a cloth before bringing it to his lips.

Tanya's soul stirred as a deep, low sound filled the air, awakening something within her that had been dormant for centuries. With eyes closed and arms outstretched, she elevated to a higher level of worship with each changing tone. Tears streamed down her face as she let go her rough exterior and surrendered to God with reverence and adoration. Benjamin skillfully closed with a series of short T'ruah blasts, concluding with one long blast, a tekiah gedolah. The sounds faded away, leaving a somber, peace-filled silence.

The couple waited patiently as Tanya finished worshiping. Alexandra handed her a tissue as she opened her eyes.

"Are you okay, my dear?" she asked.

"Yes, yes," Tanya replied, "better than I've been in a long time."

"Would you like to see Judah's writing now?" Alexandra asked.

"I would love to!" Tanya exclaimed enthusiastically.

With great care, Alexandra opened the archival box and revealed four polyester folders, each labeled with Hebrew writing. Putting on a pair of white gloves, she handled the folders delicately as if performing surgery. "Please don't touch these manuscripts," she instructed. "I will handle them and turn the pages for you."

Tanya immediately recognized her husband's distinctive style of handwriting among the Hebraic documents inside. As she read, native Hebrew flowed off her tongue in precise translation:

Athalia, you left long ago, yet it feels like yesterday. Our daughter Abigail looks more and more like you with each passing day, often reminding me of the first time I saw you. Do you remember, my love? You were in the garden picking sunflowers and laughing with Talia. I knew from the moment I saw you that you would be mine. God chose me and you for one another, He divinely appointed us, and now you are gone!

My darling, you did not have to leave. I know you would have outlived both me and our daughter, for you are bound in glory until our Savior calls you home. Although you are gone now, I know that one day you will hold this letter in your precious hands and know it is I who wrote it. My people will keep this letter and search without ceasing until you and the others are reunited. Stay strong, my love. Your time is drawing nigh.

Remember what our brother Paul said in God's sacred Word: "For in this hope we were saved. But hope that is seen is no hope at all. Who hopes for what they already have? But if we hope for what we do not yet have, we wait for it patiently."[5]

I love and long for you, so I wait patiently for that which I cannot have, knowing that our Lord with His infinite mercy will bring you back to me. Until then, that great day when His Shalom peace is ours, farewell.

Tanya wiped away the last of her tears as she finished reading the parchment. Her soul emotionally drained, she turned to the couple and asked, "Where did you get this?"

---

[5] Romans 8:24–25

We are the Essenes. We have always been part of Judaism, though hidden in the shadows. God gifts us with important missions, such as orchestrating the discovery of the dead sea scrolls of Qumran. Reuniting you and the others is our latest mission," Alexandra stated confidently.

Your husband, Judah Halevi first handed down writings about you to his friend Hafon Ha-Lev-Aldayati, whom he had many conversations with about you and two others. I don't want to bore you with the generational history and how these documents passed down to us, but rest assured they are accurate."

"I don't understand," Tanya pressed. "In my travels all over the world and over all this time, why haven't I ever met your people?" Her frustration mounted. "You obviously have some ancient documents, but how do I know those aren't fake? These days you can make anything look authentic. Why do you care so much about me and the other two? The Essenes have always practiced self-denial and austerity. Now, all of a sudden, you come out of the woodwork? I'm not going for it!"

Benjamin quickly replied, shocked and a little hurt, "Do you believe in what the wisest man to ever live said?"

"King Solomon?" Tanya asked.

"Yes," Benjamin continued. "To everything there is a time and season, and God ordains them. He orchestrates events according to His perfect will. Your time and season is now, but not without some pain and misunderstanding. My child, don't put your hope and trust in man, but in God."[6]

Tanya sighed. "I suppose you're right. I'm exhausted. I should head home." She began walking toward the door. "You obviously know where to find me."

[6] Ecclesiastes 3

CHAPTER NINETEEN

Generations

Ray's bargain with Monica temporarily masked an underlying ache. He had determined to never leave another wife, another relationship. Yet he was weary, not only in body, but in spirit. His daily prayers intensified, as did his desire to connect with God. It felt more important than ever, somehow. As he sat lost in thought, Monica's voice broke through the silence.

"Ray, I'm going to use some hair from your brush for a DNA test," she said softly.

"That's fine, honey," he replied, remembering his promise to be completely open and honest once she completed her research.

"I want to respect you and keep you informed about what I'm doing in this process," she added.

"I know," he said with a sigh.

"Could you please fill this out?" she asked, handing him a form titled "Five Generation Pedigree."

Ray took a moment to look it over—it contained a detailed, blank family tree that went back five generations. "If you'd like, I can email it to you instead," Monica offered.

"I'll take a closer look first and let you know," he said. "When do I need to return this to you?"

"The sooner the better, so I can get started," she responded before leaving the room. "Now would be great."

Ray took the form to his office and sat down at his desk, staring at it. His past was untraceable, and any information he did have was unverifiable. This would certainly raise red flags, indicating to Monica he was intentionally avoiding answers to these questions. Nonetheless, he filled in the blank spaces.

FATHER: **MOTHER:**

Born – unknown   *Born – unknown*

When – unknown   *When – unknown*

Where – unknown   *Where – unknown*

Descendants of: *unknown*

Born – unknown

Died – unknown

Married – unknown

Ray stood, clutching the completed form in his hand. He knew there would be backlash once he presented it to Monica. He made his way to her office and placed the paper on her desk. Without turning around, she reached for it and quickly spun her chair to face him.

"I had a feeling this would happen," she stated calmly, looking over the form. Ray tried not to act surprised. "I'm already one step ahead of you," she continued, standing and grabbing her purse. "I've scheduled an appointment at Anderson Lab to have your DNA tested through a hair sample." She held up a vial as proof before briskly walking out the door.

She left him standing alone with his mouth agape. But he remained confident as he sauntered into the living room and plopped down on the couch with the remote in hand. "She's got nothing," he said aloud with a smug grin. "And she's getting nothing." With that, he settled in with his popcorn and soda to watch the baseball game, not a care in the world.

CHAPTER TWENTY

The Other Two

As Tanya finished showering and changed into her pajamas, exhaustion flooded her body. She fell fast asleep as soon as her head hit the pillow. The night brought a peaceful rest, thanks to God's Shalom peace enveloping her. It defied explanation. During the conversation with Alexandra and Benjamin about Judah, Tanya felt something shifting deep inside her soul, a welcome change from her normal restlessness.

God, can we talk? It is impossible for anyone to know what it is like to live for so long. Not even my forefathers knew. Noah lived 750 years, Adam and Seth over 900 years, but I have lived longer than them all, even Methuselah at 969 years! Lord, only You know me, my ups and downs which can change by the decade or the century. I have even turned my back on You. I am not proud of this, but You have remained faithful even when I have not. Your love has been the only thing consistent in my life, and for that I am so thankful.

She slowly awakened as the sun began to filter through her window blinds. In her half-asleep state, she heard a voice whisper, *The other two.* She tried to ignore it and return to sleep, but the voice persisted, repeating the phrase. She cracked open one eye and glanced at the clock: 5:44 a.m. glared back at her in the dim room.

She groaned. *Why am I waking up so early on my day off?* She couldn't shake the intrusive thought, and when she heard "the other two" a third time, her curiosity piqued. Sitting up in bed, she remembered Alexandra mentioning her and "the other two."

I'm not imagining things. I absolutely heard you say, Lord, "The other two." Tanya immediately leapt out of bed, determined to check her magazine again. She could still recall the little boy who brought it to her as she lay on the cold concrete. *Where did I put it?* she muttered, racking her brain. She flung open her closet door and started rummaging through the torn clothes she had been wearing on the day of the accident.

"I found it!" she exclaimed, pulling out a crumpled page from under the pile of ripped jeans, pondering why she wanted to keep everything from that day together. She couldn't remember the page of the article, but she knew the title: "Man Survives 10 Days at Sea!" She flipped through the pages until she found it, eagerly scanning the article and photo. No doubt about it—he was one of the other two.

A sense of excitement bubbled up inside her as she knelt on her bedroom floor, pulling out a box from under the bed. *Two others!* she thought. She dug through its contents until she found what she was looking for: an article and photo of the *Hindenburg* disaster. *There is another guy. I saw him not long ago.* Tanya chuckled at the thought. In her mind, 1937 was recent. She had only been in the U.S. about twenty years. She had searched the crash site looking for a man, a survivor of the devastating event, but with no luck. Perhaps with help from Alexandra and Benjamin, they could finally solve the mystery.

Tanya decided to gather all the articles and magazines and bring them to the couple. They could join forces and find the other two. *Maybe I'm not alone after all.*

CHAPTER TWENTY ONE

DNA

Modern technology is a lifesaver, Monica thought as she turned on her computer. It had been a little over a month since she submitted Ray's DNA into the system.

She clicked SAVE to finalize her report, then moved the file to the designated "Ray DNA" folder. With a satisfied nod to herself, she closed her laptop and stood from her desk. In the other room, she could hear Ray shuffling around in the kitchen. The familiar ding of the microwave signaled that he was heating up leftovers for his meal. It was one of her favorite things about him—his appreciation for simplicity. Despite his high intelligence, Ray found joy in the little things in life, like reheating a homemade casserole, garlic bread on the side.

Monica greeted Ray with a warm smile as she entered the kitchen with her laptop. "How are you, babe?"

"I'm doing well, and you?" he replied.

"Fantastic!" she responded enthusiastically. "It's been a while since you've spoken with Steve," she noted as she took a seat at the dining room table next to him. "Do you have any plans set for returning to work? It's been almost two months since we were in Cairo. Do you ever see yourself going back to CCJN?"

"I want to go back, but I don't want to do an interview. Is it even legal for them to hold me hostage by making my return dependent on that?" Ray questioned.

"Most people would jump at the opportunity to be on a major network like CCJN. I'm still a little confused as to why you're against it," she pressed.

"I don't want to do it!" he responded. "And I don't have to explain myself to anyone," he added in-between bites.

"Wait a minute! I'm just anyone now?" A mix of anger and hurt sounded in her voice.

"You're not just anybody," Ray quickly clarified. "I simply don't want our lives to be put on display for the public. If I do that interview, things will never be the same for us. Remember when we first came back from Cairo? The constant presence of reporters and media camped outside our door was suffocating." *Guess my lunchtime is over. I just want some peace and quiet.*

"Ray, you have so many secrets. This hurts me and our marriage," Monica said.

He returned the microwaveable container to the refrigerator without a word. "What do you want from me, Monica?" he finally asked.

"Honesty," she responded, before he even finished speaking. She quickly opened her laptop, her perfectly manicured nails tapping away on the keyboard. She turned to him. "I want to show you something." The keyboard clicked loudly as she furiously typed. She hit RETURN with a loud slap, then spun the laptop around so he could see the screen. "Do you know what this is?" she asked, pointing at the document onscreen.

"No," Ray replied, glancing at it. "What is it?"

"It's a DNA report, Ray. Yours."

Unease washed over him as he realized the potential significance of the document. He took a closer look.

"Monica, this is all really technical stuff for someone like me. Can you explain it to me in simpler terms? What does *direct index, allele,* and *locus* mean here?"

"I'll get straight to the point," Monica said. "The report shows that you have identical DNA with at least one other person, maybe two!"

"What?" Ray exclaimed as he stood up and turned toward his wife. "That's impossible! I highly doubt a DNA sample exists for my parents anywhere. And forget about my grandparents!" Ray's agitation flared up. "What kind of joke is this?" he demanded in a loud voice. "It's not funny."

"Ray, please sit down. You're scaring me," Monica said, taken aback by the strength of his reaction, trying to calm him down. Reluctantly, he sat, looking at the screen again, visibly shaken.

"Who else out there is a closely related DNA match? How is this even possible?"

"I don't have all the answers. I just do the research and read the reports. But when I saw this news, I double- and triple-checked to ensure its accuracy. You do have a relative with closely matching DNA out there," she replied.

Ray's face fell in disbelief. "Can you find out who it is and how to reach them?"

Monica nodded. "The test showed a 99% match. I'll do some more digging and see if I can get a name or email address for you."

"Weary, I am so weary of all of this."

She placed a comforting hand on his shoulder. "It might take some time, my dear. But I promise. Whatever this means, I'll stand by your side through it all."

He managed a quiet, "Okay," as he covered his face with his hands, unable to form words.

CHAPTER TWENTY TWO

Power in
the Blood

About a month after her accident, Tanya was back on the job. Summertime in New York City was not an ideal season for sanitation workers, with garbage piling up faster than usual. Unfortunately for RJ, it was his turn to deal with the stench as Tanya drove. They had both agreed to this arrangement upon her return to work, and even though she had fully recovered, Tanya saw no harm in taking advantage of the situation as long as possible.

Tanya heard and felt RJ's *thump, thump* against the side of the truck, signaling it was time to move to the next dumpster. She slowly drove down the alleyway, reaching their next destination behind the Greek Spot.

"You want to take a break for lunch?" RJ shouted from the back of the truck.

"Sure!" she yelled back. "I'm going to go in and freshen up a bit. Are you eating here too?"

"Yeah, I'm starving," RJ responded. "I'll meet you inside."

"What's going on, girl?" Carrie called out as Tanya rushed by.

"I'll catch up with you in a minute," Tanya replied as she approached the bathroom door, the only one unlocked. She quickly washed the dirt and grime off her hands, but the smell of the city's garbage clung to her clothes. As she exited the bathroom, RJ greeted her.

"What are you doing in the men's room?" he asked, raising an eyebrow.

"Restrooms are gender-neutral nowadays, you Neanderthal," Tanya replied as she passed.

"I saved your favorite spot," Carrie said, gesturing to an isolated booth toward the back. "You and your boy are causing a disturbance for the other customers," she added pointedly, referring to their body odor.

"Oh, shut up!" Tanya said, glaring at Carrie with a side smile.

In minutes, RJ joined Tanya at the table, menu in hand. "What do you recommend?" he asked.

"You can't go wrong, RJ, no matter what you get."

"I'm keeping it simple," he replied. "Just a kabob and fries."

"Cool," Tanya said as Carrie arrived with the drinks.

As soon as they placed their order, the small talk began.

"You been following the Yankees' fast start?" Tanya asked.

"Naw, I'm a Mets fan!" RJ replied.

"I should have known," Tanya replied with a chuckle.

"I'm for the Yankees too," a voice chimed in behind Tanya. "Aaron's going to have another amazing game tonight against the Orioles' pitching staff."

"What?" Tanya turned abruptly, with attitude, to see who was talking.

The man in the booth behind her stood and apologized. "I overheard your conversation and couldn't resist joining in, as a die-hard fan myself."

"Oh, sorry!" Tanya smiled and turned back to RJ, who looked at her incredulously.

"Alright then," RJ continued, slightly annoyed as he returned to scrolling through his phone.

Their food arrived just in time. "Do you want anything else?" Carrie asked the duo.

"No, I'm good," RJ replied with a nod from Tanya across the table. Neither had realized how hungry they were until they quickly devoured their lunch. "Awesome!" he declared as he finished his last kabob and took a swig of water. "I'm ready to go. Are you?"

"Almost," Tanya said with a few bites left on her plate. "Give me a minute."

"Speaking of which, do you guys have a minute?" came the man's voice again from the other booth.

"What?" Tanya turned to see the man standing and looking at her again.

"Do you have a second?" he repeated.

"For what?" RJ interjected.

"You're the girl who got hit by a truck a few months ago, right?" the man asked.

"Who are you, another reporter?" Tanya blurted out, instantly on guard. "Well forget it!"

"Oh no, I'm not a reporter or the police," he assured them.

"Then who are you and what do you want?" Tanya demanded, angry.

"Please allow me to introduce myself. I'm Tony Hall!"

"Tony Hall. Is that supposed to mean something to me?" Tanya asked.

"Not at the moment," he responded calmly, "but if you give me a few minutes, I think it may start to mean something to you."

"Dude, you better say what you came to say!" Tanya said.

RJ took a few steps forward, ready to defend Tanya. She put her hand on his chest to stop him.

"Let's hear what he has to say first. What do you want?" Tanya demanded, as other customers began to take notice of the commotion.

"You better have a good reason for stepping up on my girl," RJ warned Tony.

"I believe we have something in common, Tanya." he said confidently. "I am one of the other ones."

His statement hit Tanya, but an inexplicable calmness washed over her. As they stood in silence, Carrie approached the group. "I remember you!" she exclaimed. "You came in here before, asking me questions about the accident. I knew you were a reporter fishing for a story. Is he bothering you, Tanya?" Carrie asked protectively. "Marc!" she yelled toward the kitchen. "Get out here and kick this bum to the curb!"

"Wait a minute!" Tanya interjected, trying to take it down a notch. "Everybody just calm down. Tony Hall, why don't you have a seat," she directed as she gestured to the booth she had just vacated.

Marc emerged from the kitchen, ready for action. The burly Greek man still wore his cooking apron, covered with various stains from work. "What's going on, Carrie?" he asked with intent.

Tanya turned to face the trio of heroes. "Everything is under control, guys. Could you give us a moment, please?"

"Are you sure?" RJ asked, still on edge.

"Yes, I'll catch up with you in a minute."

"Okay, we'll be close if you need us," Carrie said reassuringly.

"What a group," Tony commented, settling comfortably into his seat. "They obviously care about you."

"Forget about them. Who are you?" Tanya demanded.

"I don't think this is the right time or place for us to talk. Can we meet somewhere else, where it's more private?" he suggested.

"I don't know you!" Tanya exclaimed.

"Oh, but you do," Tony countered. "You just don't know it yet."

"What do you mean?" she asked, growing more impatient. "I'm tired of your games. I need to get back to work." Just then another wave of supernatural calmness washed over her. Everything seemed to move in slow motion. Turning to her left, she saw RJ head out the door with a slow gait. Turning to her right, Carrie disappeared into the kitchen with Marc. The two saloon doors closed in expanded time. A quick glance outside revealed a world nearly at standstill. *What is happening?* she wondered as the people listening in returned to eating, laughing, and joking. Tony's voice snapped Tanya out of the fog.

"Just hear me out," he persisted. A demonstration may be better than a thousand words."

Tony picked up the skewer from RJ's kabob and jammed it into his index finger. Scarlet blood trickled out. Tony used his other hand to squeeze the wound. Blood flowed freely down his finger into his palm.

"What on earth are you doing?" Tanya whispered. "Are you a psycho or something?" she added for good measure.

"Just watch," Tony replied calmly, holding up his blood-covered finger for her to see. He grabbed several napkins from the dispenser and started wiping away the blood from his palm and finger. Tanya watched in amazement as the wound stopped bleeding and began to heal. The hole in Tony's finger slowly closed up, while the damaged tissue regenerated itself until it looked as good as new. Tony showed off his healed finger like a magician showing off his latest trick.

Before she could ask any questions, he quickly cleaned up the rest of the blood with water-soaked napkins and excused himself to go to the bathroom. Once there, he disposed of all the evidence of his little demonstration before returning to their table.

Tanya was still in shock.

"Why are you surprised?" he asked.

Then quick as a flash of lightning, Tony grabbed the skewer and poked Tanya in the palm of her hand with it.

"Ouch!" she exclaimed, as blood began to trickle from the small wound. Tony quickly handed her some napkins from the dispenser, watching as each napkin soaked up the blood. As the last tissue turned red, Tony quickly grabbed hold of Tanya's hand and inspected the puncture wound. She tried to pull away, but Tony's grip was too strong. He watched as her hand stopped bleeding, and layer by layer, the skin repaired itself. Within minutes her palm appeared 90 percent healed. Using water-soaked napkins, he carefully wiped away any traces of blood until nothing remained on Tanya's hand.

He apologized once more before standing to dispose of the napkins in the men's restroom bin. When he returned, he found Tanya's expression stoic. She willfully hid her excitement as she pondered the event, knowing why Tony looked so familiar to her.

"Open up your phone and give it to me," she demanded. He complied and handed over his phone, then watched as she quickly found his number and entered it into her phone, texting him. *Tony, this is Tanya Bloom. Don't come back here again. I'll be in touch.* And with that, she got up and walked out the door.

CHAPTER TWENTY THREE

The J-O-B

Two-plus months after his return from Cairo, Ray finally felt strong enough to return to work. The media frenzy that had surrounded his homecoming had died down, and the once sensationalized "Cairoman" became yesterday's news.

Ray and Monica were getting along smoothly, although Ray could tell his wife was on a mission to uncover his family history. The media had finally left the Witt household, so the couple often went on walks together, but not today.

Ray reached for his cell phone to call Steve. He wanted to discuss the possibility of returning to work soon. Monica was in her office, busy with a business call. Ray scrolled through his contacts until he found Steve's personal number.

As the phone rang, uneasiness washed over him. He and Steve had been colleagues for fifteen years, but something about this call felt different. Too many questions had gone unanswered since their time in Egypt. Steve wondered about Ray's miraculous survival, without a single visible wound or injury on his body. *Maybe it would be best just to avoid this call and stay home,* Ray considered. A voice on the other end of the line suddenly interrupted his thoughts.

"Steve Moore speaking," the voice said, bringing Ray back to reality.

"Hey Steve, it's Ray. Did my name not show up on your caller ID?" he asked.

"Hey Ray, how are you?" Steve replied, avoiding the question.

"I'm doing well. How about you, Theresa, and the family?" Ray asked politely.

"Everyone is great. And how is Monica?" Steve inquired.

"She's doing well," he answered, ending the small talk. "Listen, Steve. I think I'm ready to come back to work. I feel healthy and even a little eager."

"Really?" came the response from the other end. "We've had many discussions here about your return, and what that would look like," Steve replied.

"What does that mean?" Ray questioned. "Do I still have a job at CCJN?"

"Of course, Ray," Steve assured him. "But there are some details we still need to iron out."

"Like what?" he pressed.

"On the flight back from Cairo, we were trying to get some answers from you, but you were too exhausted to provide them. Do you remember that?"

"Not really," Ray admitted, bracing himself for what he knew was coming next.

"Ray, the network is requesting an exclusive interview with you before you talk to any other media outlets about what happened in Cairo. You are a miraculous survivor of an event that claimed over 300,000 lives. People around the globe, as well as here in our own country, are eager to meet the "Cairoman" and hear your story firsthand. As someone in the news industry, I'm sure you can appreciate the interest, right?"

Ray hesitated before responding to the loaded question. "I suppose so, Steve," he finally replied reluctantly. "Are you implying that my return is contingent on me doing this interview?"

"It's not my call, Ray. It's coming from higher up," Steve insisted.

"You knew when you hired me that I wanted a career behind the camera, not in front of it," Ray argued.

"I understand that. But think about it from the network's perspective. You're a gold mine, not just now but for years to come. We're willing to change your job description and offer you a raise with a new contract. We only need you to sign exclusively with us," Steve countered.

"Do you actually think I'm shopping my story out to other networks?" Steve paused before answering.

"So much has happened to you and the network in the past couple of months. No one around here is sure what anyone else is doing or thinking. We all just want to get on the same page," Steve said with compassion.

"I'm honestly shaken, disturbed, and hurt by the network's actions. I'll need some time to think about what you've said. And I want to talk to Monica about it."

"Since you were on the job when everything happened, you still have three more weeks of workman's comp due to you. Can we revisit this conversation at the end of the week?"

"Okay, sure," Ray agreed, then heard the click of Steve's phone.

With the issue unresolved, Ray returned to his office a week later, and everything appeared exactly as he had left it, not even a pencil out of place. As he settled into his chair, one by one, his colleagues came in to greet him and welcome him back. It felt refreshing to be out of the house and back at work. Ray powered on his computer and patiently waited for the login screen to appear.

Mark burst into the room with a loud greeting. "Welcome back, my friend! How's it going, Ray? Or should I say 'Cairoman'?"

Ray looked up at Mark. "Ray is doing well." With that, he redirected his attention to his computer.

"Sorry, Ray," Mark said sheepishly. "I thought you were okay with the nickname. How are you feeling?"

"I'm doing well," he answered, a bit overwhelmed by all the attention. "Just a little anxious, not knowing what to expect," he admitted. "I'm taking things slowly. How's Liz and the family?"

"They're all good," Mark reassured him. "Liz will be coming by later this afternoon. Maybe she'll stop by and say hi."

"That would be fine."

"Okay, man. I have to get going. Will I see you at the staff meeting at 10:00?" Mark asked.

"Yes, I'll be there," he confirmed. "See you then."

"Yep," Mark replied as he left the doorway. Ray dreaded the upcoming meeting, the questions he didn't want to answer.

The bustling commotion of the office pulled his attention away from the computer again—people in constant motion, some holding coffee, others with papers and laptops in hand. Live news feeds from all over the world flashed across multiple TV screens. Ray couldn't help but feel a twinge of nostalgia for the fast-paced environment he used to thrive in. But now, as someone who had become the subject of the news, he wanted nothing to do with it. Lost in thought, he didn't even notice when Steve appeared at his doorway.

"Hey, Ray. How are you doing?" he asked warmly as he approached with his hand outstretched. Ray stood to shake his boss's hand.

"I'm doing well, Steve," he replied, still standing.

"It's great to have you back. The office hasn't been the same without you," Steve said sincerely. "I hope you've recovered from all the chaos and drama in Cairo. That was a lot to handle. Hopefully things have settled down for you now."

"Yeah, things are much better now. Thanks for your kind words," Ray responded gratefully.

"Just a heads up: We have a staff meeting in an hour, and I want to let you know that you're on the agenda. As we discussed on the flight back from Cairo, people are eager to hear from the Cairoman. You may prefer to remain anonymous, but I don't think that's possible." Ray sat, listening quietly as Steve spoke. After a pause, he continued, explaining, "It all comes down to who breaks the story first," he said, looking directly at Ray. "We want you to share your experience with the earthquake and its aftermath through our platform, in your own words and with the assistance of our team."

Ray slowly sank back into his chair and turned his attention to his laptop. Carefully, he entered his login credentials and waited for the homepage to load. "Steve," he said, still focused on his screen, "I'm still curious. If I don't agree to do this interview, will my job at CCJN be in jeopardy?"

"That's not a fair question, Ray," Steve replied, taking a seat in front of Ray's desk. "Think about it from our perspective—which should also be yours. You were trapped under rubble for five days during an earthquake and miraculously survived unscathed. The world wants to hear your story, so yes, your job is on the line," Steve replied emphatically as he leaned toward Ray. "Our higher-ups believe that if you decline the interview with us, it means you've probably already signed with another station for more money than what we're paying you now." Now, Steve's words didn't faze Ray in the slightest. "Can you see where we're coming from?" asked Steve.

"I understand completely, Steve. In fact, I may understand more than you realize. After all, Monica and I will be the ones whose lives are forever changed."

"Have you discussed it with her?"

"We've talked about it extensively," retorted Ray. "In her own way, Monica agrees with you that I should share my story publicly."

"So, what's holding you back?" Steve asked sympathetically.

"There is no hesitation on my end," Ray stated firmly.

"So you'll do it?" asked Steve excitedly, standing up from his chair again.

"Of course I will. And where better to share my story than here with my CCJN news family?"

"I'll see you in 45 minutes, then." Steve checked his watch before heading to the door. Ray returned to his computer and the 110 unread emails waiting in his inbox.

As soon as Ray walked in, Monica could tell something was wrong by the look on his face. He hurriedly sat down on the couch and turned to her.

"They want me to do a mini-series, a documentary about my time in Cairo. The legal team was present during our meeting. They're afraid I'll sell my story to the highest bidder."

"None of this seems legal," Monica assured him. "Have you spoken to a lawyer about it?"

"No, but let's wait until tomorrow morning to talk more when we're well-rested and can think more clearly."

"How about dinner then?" Monica suggested.

"Sure," Ray agreed as he got up and headed toward the bedroom. He took off his coat and tie and hung them in the closet. As he put his shoes on the rack, he noticed his suitcase sitting on the top shelf and felt his fight or flight instincts kick in. He had left situations in the past countless times when his true identity was at risk. He had reached that point again.

A weight suddenly descended on his chest and spread throughout his body, gently collapsing him to the floor. He couldn't make a sound. The sensation rushed to his head; weight bore down on him as if an elephant sat on top of him. This was no stroke or heart attack, but something else entirely. He remained motionless, but not paralyzed. He didn't want to move.

He felt no pain, he simply existed. This sensation was familiar to him, a feeling of nothingness, where time and space held no importance; complete rest and peace prevailed. Suddenly, a soft voice broke through the stillness:

Stay with Monica. Then, the heaviness dissipated—first in his head, then his limbs, torso, arms, shoulders, chest, and finally his spirit. He rolled onto his back and remained there for what seemed like eternity. Indescribable tranquility and joy flooded his soul.

I understand, Ray whispered. *I'll do what you say.* He repeated the words over and over, caught between two worlds. Reality crashed in on him as Monica called out, "Ray, dinner is ready!" And just like that, he returned from this heavenly state.

Ray held a script detailing the questions his interviewer would ask, but he couldn't shake off his nerves. Sitting in the green room for the first time only added to his anxiety. He'd be on air in about fifteen minutes. The makeup team had already left, leaving him and Monica alone in the small space.

"How are you feeling?" Monica asked.

"Honestly, like I'm about to expose our entire life to the public. From now on, we'll never have a private moment in public again. I'm sorry they wouldn't let you join me on stage. We would have made an amazing team."

"I know. But you'll do great. I have faith in you!" she reassured him.

"Would you pray for me?" Ray asked earnestly.

"Of course." Monica's hand found its place in his. "Heavenly Father, we come to You now with a simple request, to be with Ray in this interview. Let his words be a powerful testimony of Your saving grace, so others may see that You are always present and active in the lives of Your people. Give him courage and confidence to speak truth to a world in need of hope. Bless your child, Rayford Witt, today! Amen."

"Come here," Ray said, standing to embrace his wife.

A knock on the door interrupted them. "Ray, you're up in five minutes," came a voice from outside. He opened the door to find an assistant waiting for them.

"Right this way, sir," a man in his thirties said, leading Ray and Monica to a backstage entrance. The lights were blinding, and Ray could see four cameras with boom microphones. In the center of it all sat two sofa-style chairs separated by a sleek coffee table.

A well-dressed woman approached Ray and unbuttoned his coat, slipping a small black receiver into his inner pocket before clipping a lapel mic on his suit jacket. "I'm Linda Morgan, the assistant director. Mr. Witt, please take a seat in that chair, stage left," she gestured.

"Mrs. Witt, if you follow me this way," she continued, walking away.

Ray and Monica's eyes locked, and without exchanging words, they lovingly kissed. Ms. Morgan turned and realized Monica wasn't behind her. She pushed her trendy glasses up on her nose and gestured for Monica to follow her.

A tall man in his forties entered from the other side and reached out his hand to shake Ray's. "Hello, Ray. My name is Benson, and I'll be your director."

"See that man walking around and giving orders? That's the producer, Mr. Russell," Benson said, pointing to a short, balding man with a busy demeanor. "Don't expect him to have much to say; he prefers to be down here instead of up in the booth. I'll be your main point of contact and make sure everything runs smoothly. Please, take a seat," he gestured.

Just then, Devon Vinson walked into the studio. As CCJN's top anchorman, everyone knew him. He carried himself with polished confidence, dressed impeccably and groomed to perfection. Two people were still fussing over him as he entered. He held a script in his hand. Ray could hear him rehearsing his lines with varying voice inflections.

Oh boy! Ray thought. *Man, I really dislike pretentious people.*

"Devon, this is Ray Witt," Benson introduced him. Without looking up from his script, Devon responded in a rehearsed tone, "Nice to meet you," then promptly took his seat

Monica, sitting with Linda behind the bright lights, watched the exchange with interest. "Help him out, Jesus," she whispered under her breath.

"Now Ray, we're recording this session to air later," Benson informed him. "Ideally, we'd like to do it all in one take, but if needed, we can do another. Understand?"

"Yeah, sure," he responded casually. *Does he not realize that I've been on countless sets and shoots?*

"We're going live in two minutes. Everyone to their places," Benson announced. The room erupted into a frenzy as everyone scrambled to the ready. A female voice beside the director's chair called out, "Quiet on set." Another chimed in: "Picture is up." Benson followed suit with "Roll sound," and "Roll cameras." Pointing to Devon, he declared: "Slate . . . Action!"

"Welcome, everyone. This is Devon Vinson reporting from CCJN headquarters in New York City. Today, we have a very special guest joining us, Mr. Rayford Witt, one of our own at CCJN. Ray was recently on assignment in the great city of Cairo, Egypt when a 9.0 earthquake struck."

Why did I decide to go through with this? Ray wondered, as Devon continued his introduction. The glaring lights and monotonous sound of Devon's voice made him question it all again. Then peace washed over him—just as he had felt in his bedroom a few days prior.

A familiar voice spoke to his spirit once more, reassuring him: *I'll help you.*

Monica gazed at Ray's expressionless face, worried. *What's going on with him? I've never seen him look like this before. I hope everything's okay.*

"Ladies and gentlemen, let me introduce our special guest today—Rayford Witt." His announcement snapped Ray back to reality. "Ray, welcome to the show. Let's begin by hearing about your recent experience in Cairo. What was it like to go through such an intense earthquake?"

"It was absolutely terrifying," answered Ray. "I wouldn't wish that on anyone."

"Where were you when it happened?" Devon asked the question on everyone's mind. The answer would either make his story believable or spark further investigation.

"To be honest, Devon, it's a bit of a blur for me. I think I was walking toward an elevator. But when the building started shaking, I believe I ran toward the stairs."

Devon didn't expect that answer. He followed up with the next prepared question on his list. "Do you believe that decision saved your life?"

"Apparently so," Ray responded without hesitation. He didn't offer any more information, and Devon's attitude shifted dramatically.

"Cut!" Benson yelled in frustration. He turned to Ray and pleaded, "We need more from you than just one-word responses. It's crucial that you elaborate on Devon's questions." Benson rubbed his bald head in exasperation. "Understand?"

"I do," Ray simply replied. Benson then turned to Linda. "What was that last question from Devon?" The voice behind the lights repeated, "Do you believe that decision saved your life?" Benson nodded and exclaimed, "Alright, let's continue!" He directed everyone back to their places. "And Action!" Devon posed his question once more, directing it at Ray and turning his chair toward him for emphasis.

"I recall falling and being tossed around in midair. Debris and metal were raining down on me. The noise was haunting! Like a scene from *The Wizard of Oz*, when Dorthy was sitting in her bed and a tornado swept her away as people and objects swirled around her." Ray continued to recall his nightmare experience.

"So, you witnessed people falling to their deaths?" Devon inquired.

"I believe so," Ray answered hesitantly. "How could I not? The hotel was packed with people and hotel personnel. The death screams were deafening."

"What happened after you reached the ground?" Devon questioned, checking his notes.

"According to our files, your room was on the 42nd floor of the hotel. Yet, the medical report shows no broken bones or even a sprained ankle. How is that possible, Ray?" Devon probed further.

Ray shifted uncomfortably in his seat. "I can't make sense of it any more than you or anyone else," he replied confidently, then threw another curveball: "Do you believe in divine intervention?" The dynamics of the interview shifted again.

"CUT!" Benson yelled from behind the lights. Devon stood up, his arms raised in confusion. Benson hurried over to the stage, and Devon turned to him, asking, "What's going on?"

Benson looked visibly upset. "Ray, you can't ask a question like that. You're supposed to answer questions, not ask them."

"I'm simply proposing an answer to an unanswerable question, based on logic—"

"Stop!" Benson interrupted before he could finish. "This interview is not about faith, God, or supernatural occurrences," Benson clarified as Ray tried to interrupt again.

"For you, maybe. But for me, it is! If you want me to talk about my experience, then let's do it. But if you want me to analyze and dissect every moment of it, then that will be my answer," Ray responded firmly.

His response took Benson aback. "What the hell?" he muttered under his breath.

Ray remained calm. "Sir, this isn't about hell. In fact, it's quite the opposite."

Monica couldn't contain her amusement and chuckled from her seat.

Addressing Benson directly, Ray asked, "What do you want to do?"

Before he could answer, Mr. Russell made his way into the chaotic scene. "I'll answer that! Devon! You and the writers have two hours to revise the questions and come up with better wording. Otherwise, you're all fired!"

Turning to anyone listening, he shouted, "Break!"

CHAPTER TWENTY FOUR

Tamar and the Levite

After a long day at work, Tanya felt conflicted over her encounter with Tony. She was relieved to know she wasn't the only one with extraordinary powers; her unique ability often overwhelmed her with no one to confide in. The thought of sharing it with someone who could truly comprehend her indestructible nature excited her. Someone who also had watched loved ones age and pass away while he remained unchanged. *Would he be willing to share his experiences with her?* As she sat down on her couch and opened her phone, she considered all the possibilities that lay ahead.

She looked at Tony's contact information. *Hmmm, he doesn't look like a Tony. He seems more like an Isaac, Asher, or Caleb.* After years of living on different continents and experiencing different cultures, Tanya considered herself an expert on reading people. She had possessed plenty of time and experience to hone this skill. *Eventually, the mystery of his true character will reveal itself,* she thought. After a few sips of tea, she decided to call Dr. Abrams and tell her about the encounter. She scrolled through her contacts until she found Alexandra's name, tapping on it to call her.

After three rings, a voice answered on the other end. "Hello Tanya, how are you?"

"Hello, doctor," Tanya replied. "I'm doing well, but my hand is a bit sore."

"Your hand? Why?"

"Well, that's actually why I'm calling you," Tanya admitted. "I've met one of the other two." The line went silent as Dr. Abrams processed the information. "Doctor? Are you there?"

"Yes, I'm here."

"Did you hear what I said?" Tanya repeated.

"Yes, yes, I heard you," she replied, tearing up at the news.

"Are you crying?" Tanya asked with concern.

"Just a little," Alexandra managed. "Tanya, we have spent our entire lives searching for you and the other two. Praise God that our journey may soon come to an end. And when I say 'our' journey, I mean yours too.

"You are opening up again to the things of God. God is able to reveal things to you that your flesh and blood cannot understand, but your spirit does. This is both the start and the end—the start of you understanding your purpose from ancient days and the end of your journey." Her words held a sense of finality, causing Tanya's heart to race with anticipation. "Were you touched by the Master?"

Tanya's voice filled with exhaustion as she spoke. "Yes, and I'm so tired, not just physically, to where I feel pain much longer now. I'm emotionally drained."

"It must be overwhelming," Alexandra replied sympathetically. "I cannot even begin to understand, but Jesus knows, and He cares. Your breakthrough is coming soon, and you will once again feel God's power in a special way!"

"Yes . . . yes!" Tanya managed to say between deep breaths.

"Now tell me about the other one. I'm putting you on speaker phone so my husband can hear."

"Well, he looked very Jewish," Tanya began, "but he introduced himself as Tony Hall."

"Tony Hall?" came a male voice through the phone. "I've never heard of him," Benjamin added.

"Of course not," Alexandra replied. "Let her continue."

"My apologies," Benjamin said.

"How did you meet and how do you know he is one of 'the other ones'?" Alexandra asked.

Tanya shared her encounter at the diner, and as they discussed it further, God's presence stirred among them, bringing a fresh energy and ushering in new beginnings. Tanya hung up the phone, then decided to call Tony.

As he worked on replacing the air filtration system on the PT6 turbine engine, Tony felt his phone vibrate in his pocket. He paused for a moment, taking a quick break from working on his friend Adam's crop duster. He carefully set the engine cover down and took out his phone, seeing "Tanya Bloom" on the screen.

Tony answered. "Can you hold on a minute, Tanya?"

"Of course," she replied.

Tony placed his phone down and headed to the sink to wash off some of the grease and dirt from his hands and arms. After cleaning up, he returned to the wing of the plane and picked up his phone again.

"How are you?" he inquired. "Has your hand fully recovered?"

"That's hilarious," Tanya replied sarcastically. "I'm fine, and yourself?"

"I'm great!" Tony exclaimed. "What can I do for you?"

"Well, I was wondering when and where we could meet privately to discuss some important matters. I also want to introduce you to a special couple," Tanya said.

"Really? You told someone else about yourself? he asked, shocked. "I'm confused. Why would you do that? Are they like us?" he asked with surprise.

"They're not like us."

"Then why did you tell them?"

Tanya felt her old self resurfacing, but the new-and-improved version—thanks to God's grace—stayed calm and took a few deep breaths before answering. "This couple found me, and they know everything about me—things I haven't shared with anyone else. They possess books, scrolls, and other ancient writings that contain information about me. And probably you too."

"That doesn't make sense to me either," he replied.

"Have you ever heard of the Essenes?"

He took a moment to think before responding, intrigued by her words. "The group from the Tribe of Levi? The sect that died out after John the Baptist?" Tony inquired.

"Yes, but they didn't die out," Tanya quickly interjected.

"What do you mean?"

"These two are Essenes." Matter-of-fact in tone, Tanya informed him, "You are from the tribe of Levi."

He stood in shock. "How do you know that?" he asked, clearly troubled.

"They told me," Tanya answered confidently. "I also know that you were a pilot—not just any pilot, but the one flying the *Hindenburg*! Does May 6, 1937, ring a bell? That's when you first came to America from Germany." Tanya's words stunned him. He made his way to the nearest vacant office to sit and process it all.

"Did they tell you about that too?"

"No, I witnessed it myself. I saw everything."

"What?"

"Yes, I went by Kim then, but that doesn't matter. What matters is that you were there! I went to witness the Zepplin land, and I saw the first sparks as the tail section burst into flames. I watched as the fire spread to the front of the aircraft, and I saw you trying your best to land it."

Tony sat in silence, listening intently.

"Once the balloon crashed, I saw something else through all the smoke, fumes, and gas—you, running out of the flames. Your uniform was burning on your body. I tried to catch you, but you were way too fast for me, maybe because you were on fire or you were just naturally fast. That day you met me at the café, I thought I recognized you. God did something special in me that day. Everything slowed and a fog lifted off me, otherwise I never would have spoken with you. I didn't say anything, but I will never forget you. Fire, smoke, beard or no beard! This couple may know of you, but I know you too!" Tanya continued.

"You're correct," Tony began, "I did help pilot the Zeppelin. I had just finished chatting with actor Gig Young before heading back to the flight deck." Tony began speaking in fluent German as he recounted the events that followed.

Tanya listened awhile before trying to get his attention. "Tony," then louder, "Tony!"

"What?!" he snapped back.

"You're speaking in German!"

After a moment of confusion, he continued on in English without skipping a beat. "As Captain Max piloted through the headwinds and mild thunderstorms, everything seemed to be under control. Then, a spark ignited a fire in the tail section of the ship. It spread quickly, engulfing the entire vessel in less than a minute. Most of the passengers and crew jumped out the front windows on the promenade deck. I helped a woman and her two sons jump to safety, but then my own clothes caught fire, and I began burning. Once we landed, I ran as fast as I could away from the ship. That must have been when you saw me.

"I stumbled on a hangar at the far end of the airfield and found a run-down office inside where I could rest and recover." He sighed. "I had first-, second-, and third-degree burns covering my body. Probably the worst injury I had ever experienced, until recently."

"Recently?"

"Yes. I had a recent run-in with a jet engine in a hangar again, no less. It mangled me," he recounted sadly.

"Do you want to talk about it? You know I understand, right?" Tanya asked softly, with a clear shift in her disposition.

"Yes, I know you do," he replied. "Not right now. I'm wondering more where we go from here?"

CHAPTER TWENTY FIVE

Shared DNA

Monica had no interest in accompanying Ray to his second day of shooting. "Do you need me to join you today?" she asked Ray while applying her makeup.

"I don't think so, Moni," he replied. "Most of the excitement is over and the final interviews should go smoothly. Why? What's going on?"

"I have some follow-up work to do on a DNA report. My appointment is at 11:00 a.m."

"I have some work to finish after the interview," Ray mentioned. "I'll text you when I have a better idea of when I'll be home."

"Sounds like a plan," Monica agreed.

Ray embraced her from behind, whispering, "I love you" against her neck as he planted kisses on her cheek.

Monica giggled and pushed him away, playfully. "I love you too, but you're going to make me late!" she scolded with a smile.

"Aye aye, Captain," he replied with a grin before heading out the door.

Monica quickly finished getting ready. She started the car and put her destination address into the navigation system, dreading the traffic in the city. After an hour and fifteen minutes, she finally arrived, pulling into a department store parking lot. She walked a few blocks to Norwood Street, then scanned the names on the panel until she found "Abrams." She pressed the intercom button and waited for a response.

"Yes?" came a voice from the other end. "May I help you?"

"My name is Monica Witt, and we spoke on the phone about some matching DNA."

"Come on up," the voice said, and the door buzzed open.

Monica took the elevator to the fourth floor. As she stepped off, a woman stood in her doorway, beckoning her inside and extending her hand. "This way, please."

"Hello, I am Dr. Abrams, or Alexandra," she introduced herself.

"Nice to meet you. I'm Monica Witt."

"Please come in, Monica. This is my husband, Benjamin," Alexandra gestured.

"Thank you for having me. It's a pleasure to meet both of you."

"Can I get you something to drink?" Benjamin offered.

"Yes please. Water is fine," Monica accepted. "So, what kind of doctor are you?" she asked Alexandra conversationally.

"I'm an MD in the emergency room in midtown New York. And yourself?"

"Oh, I'm a genealogist. That's why I'm here."

"Indeed," Benjamin chimed in. "We were actually expecting and searching for a male relative."

"Let me interject, please," Alexandra interrupted. "You contacted me and mentioned that you had found a sibling match with a sample I had submitted to our database. Is that accurate?"

"Not exactly," Monica said. "I have both DNA and SNP matches with a sample you entered into the DNA database. So, the match isn't necessarily a sibling. It is a close relative."

"So, who is the match exactly?" Benjamin asked.

"It's my husband, Ray," Monica revealed with a heavy sigh. "Lately, he's been acting strangely and saying things that don't make any sense."

"What kind of things?" Benjamin asked, intrigued.

Confidence radiated from Monica as she spoke. "You may have heard of him. He's known as Cairoman."

"Who?" the couple asked in unison, turning to each other with puzzled expressions.

"Ray was in Cairo, Egypt during the 9.0 earthquake earlier this year. He was staying in a high-rise hotel when it struck. He miraculously survived under the wreckage for five days and nights, without so much as a scratch on him," Monica explained. "That's how he earned the nickname Cairoman. But ever since then, he's been acting strangely and keeping secrets from me. Ray has always contended that he has no family, and this has always been a sore point in our marriage. In my business I have found that everyone has someone. Every holiday is spent with my family, which is now our abnormal norm. He never mentions childhood birthdays or Christmas memories, nothing . . . It's just weird! Now, for the first time in our lives, a door is opening to Ray's family and his past. I plan to open that door!"

She paused looking intently at the couple. "Ray works for CCJN, and they're airing his story next week. You must watch it! Anyway, what do you think?"

"About the DNA match or the upcoming interview?" Alexandra asked.

"Both," Monica quickly replied, sensing coyness in the couple.

Benjamin replied, "We'll definitely tune in to watch the interview, but I'll have to defer to my wife regarding the DNA matches."

Alexandra moved on. "I submitted the DNA of a young woman who we know personally. We may have some theories of how it could closely match with your husband's, because our match is unique. If you give me the paperwork, I'll look it over. Then I'll be in a better position to comment on it."

"That makes sense," Monica said before concluding the conversation. "Can you help us?"

Benjamin rose from his seat and reached out to shake Monica's hand. "Yes, I believe we can," he replied confidently. Monica stood and shook his hand as she headed to the door. Turning one final time with a nod, she disappeared down the hallway.

"Benjamin, why did you tell her we can help her?" Alexandra scolded. "We don't have enough evidence to prove he is like the other two."

Benjamin asked, "What do you think about the DNA match?"

Without hesitation, she replied, "I think it no longer is a scientific question but a spiritual one. It's time to pray!"

CHAPTER TWENTY SIX

Shabbat Shalom

Tanya became a regular visitor at the Abrams household, forming a close bond with the couple. It had been so long since she had the presence of a stable parental figure in her life. She didn't realize how much she yearned for their leadership, guidance, and wisdom. On one of these visits, she received a surprising invitation.

"Tanya, we would like to invite you to our Shabbat Christian Fellowship Center," Alexandra proposed.

"Why?" Tanya questioned out of curiosity.

"Because you have only interacted with us, but there are many others who played crucial roles in finding you, and in finding the other two. Historians, biblical experts, and prayerful intercessors are just a few of the members on our team. We want to share our history with you, update you on the current situation with all three of you, and discuss what we think the next steps should be," Alexandra explained.

"I think I understand," Tanya replied, "but what about Tony and the third person?"

"Well, that's why we asked you to come here today," Benjamin explained. "Did you bring all of your magazines and articles with you?"

"Yes, they're in my backpack," Tanya confirmed as she emptied its contents on the coffee table.

"Perfect!" Alexandra exclaimed.

"We have something for you to watch." Benjamin picked up the remote from the end table.

"Are you ready?" Alexandra asked.

"I suppose so," Tanya answered nervously as images appeared on the television.

> *Welcome, everyone. This is Devon Vinson reporting from CCJN headquarters in New York City. Today, we have a very special guest joining us, Mr. Rayford Witt, one of our own at CCJN. Ray was recently on assignment in the great city of Cairo, Egypt when a 9.0 earthquake struck.*

As the camera panned away from Devon, Tanya froze.

> *Ray, welcome to the show.*

Devon greeted him with a smile as the camera zoomed in on Ray's face.

Tanya suddenly interrupted. "Stop it! Pause it! I know him! I know him!"

Benjamin paused the close-up shot of Rayford Witt's face.

Tanya frantically searched through the magazines and articles scattered on the coffee table.

"I found him!" she exclaimed, holding up an article from a dumpster. "It's him! Look, it's him! Leonardo, the man I once knew in Italy!" She jumped up from the couch and held the magazine picture next to the frozen image of Ray on the screen.

"Yes, it is him," Alexandra confirmed. "He is the other one, the missing one."

"Are you sure?" she asked with disbelief, continuing her animated behavior. "Why aren't you more surprised? How are you so certain?"

"Please, Tanya, can you sit down for a moment?" Alexandra interrupted. "We met Ray's wife. Her name is Monica."

The news confused Tanya. "I don't understand."

"Ray's wife is a genealogist, and she matched your DNA with Ray's," Alexandra explained. "Your family DNA is a match."

Tanya gasped in shock. "Nooo! I have so many questions. For starters, I've never given anyone my blood for DNA testing. How could we possibly be a match?"

Dr. Abrams hung her head in shame. "It was me, child," she admitted. "When I treated you that day at the hospital, I couldn't shake my suspicions about your quickly healing injuries. I secretly took a sample of your blood and ran it through various genealogical databases."

"What?! Is that even legal?" she asked.

"No, it's not," the doctor confessed. "If you report me, I could lose my medical license." Tears welled up in her eyes. "So many of us have devoted our lives to finding you three. I guess I just let desperation cloud my judgement."

Tanya's initial anger faded as she realized the gravity of the situation. This was bigger than her, the doctor, or even their group. God had intention in all of it. She stood and embraced Alexandra, both of them crying softly together.

Mr. Abrams switched off the television, deep in prayer, contemplating the events that had just unfolded. The palpable shift in their lives was part of a greater plan, divine intervention, an act of God. That day changed them all in ways they could never imagine.

In only a few days after visiting Benjamin and Alexandra, Tanya stepped through the doors of their place of worship for a special ceremony, her first experience at a Messianic Jewish event. *What an interesting blend of Judaism and Christianity,* she thought.

In many ways, it felt as if she had just entered a synagogue. A prayer wall stood to the left, modeled after the Western Wall in Jerusalem; a beautiful purple tapestry presented the menorah embroidered in gold; and the centerpiece of the sanctuary—a huge Star of David—encompassed a gold crucifix at its center, handcrafted from wood, outlined with a stunning blue malachite stone, or "Malachi Blue."

Tanya's eyes scanned the stage, taking in the keyboard, drum set, and guitar on stands, as well as an American and Israeli flag side by side. *This is definitely not your typical traditional Jewish setup,* she noted.

Alexandra greeted her as she entered, walking her to a seat at the front where she met Rabbi Nathaniel Cohn, an attractive man in his forties wearing a polo, black slacks, and a jacket.

"It's a pleasure to meet you, Rabbi," Tanya said.

"Shabbat Shalom. The pleasure is all mine," he replied with a warm smile. "We have prayed for this day for many years, and now it has finally come. To God be the glory! How are you holding up, Tanya?" he asked with concern. "I can only imagine how much your life has been turned upside down recently."

"I'm managing," she replied, her voice heavy with exhaustion. "With all the new information and changes coming so quickly, it's been a lot to process."

"I can understand that." Rabbi Cohn grasped her hands reassuringly, then casually gestured toward the musicians, who were picking up their instruments.

A woman called out, "Let us all stand as we worship Yeshua, our Lord and Savior."

Tanya had never heard these songs before, but the blend of instruments sounded so sweet and inviting. The lyrics appeared onscreen at the back of the stage, so she joined in, singing with everyone else. She hardly realized as one song seamlessly transitioned to the next. Her heart filled with joy, simply from the opportunity to sing and rejoice with her people.

Then it happened. The band broke out with "Hava Nagila," a traditional Jewish pizmonim,[7] uniting everyone. People young and old jumped out of their seats and circled the front of the sanctuary, dancing with arms raised, singing, "Hava, Hava Nagila / Hava nagila, vnismecha."

The Rabbi turned to Tanya. "You know this song, Tamar, don't you? It's as old as you are," he winked, then quickly recovered from his faux pas. "Why don't you join us?" He reached out and took her hand. She took hold of his handkerchief and joined him on the makeshift dance floor as they sang, "Let us, Let us rejoice / Let us rejoice and be happy!"

Amidst the crowd, men wearing traditional kippahs[8] and women with scarfs and sheitels[9] danced and twirled in a large circle. Tanya effortlessly joined in, remembering every move she had learned in childhood. It had been a long time since she had enjoyed herself so much with fellow Jews.

The band's tempo increased, and the congregation moved along with the pulsing rhythm. Men and women stepped, tapped, and twisted in unison, circling in one direction before reversing course. And then, with a single triumphant cry of "Halleluiah!" it ended.

---

[7] Traditional Jewish songs/melodies meant for praising God and teaching religious truth. Wikipedia, accessed June 4, 2025, https://en.wikipedia.org/wiki/Pizmonim.

[8] kippah: A typically cloth Jewish skullcap worn by Jewish men to honor the Torah's requirement for covering the head. Wikipedia, accessed June 4, 2025, https://en.wikipedia.org/wiki/Kippah.

[9] sheitel: A wig or half-wig worn by married Jewish women to honor the requirement for covering their hair around men who aren't close family members. Wikipedia, accessed June 4, 2025, https://en.wikipedia.org/wiki/Head_covering_for_Jewish_women.

As the people cheered, Rabbi Cohn made his way to the microphone. "Haleluye!" he exclaimed again and again. He greeted the crowd with "Shalom," and in unison they replied, "And Shalom to you as well!"

"Brothers and sisters, tonight we celebrate what Jesus has done in our lives, and our special guest: Tamar of Galilee!"

Tanya was at ease, unfazed by the sudden attention.

"Our service will be brief tonight as myself and some of the elders must attend to important matters concerning Tamar and two others. Elder Benowitz will provide further details and announcements."

The rabbi stepped down from the stage and led the Abrams, Tanya, and three other people (whom she didn't recognize) down the aisle. People stood and leaned in toward her, wanting to touch her. She happily greeted everyone within reach with a handshake, fist bump, or high five.

CHAPTER TWENTY SEVEN

Revelation—Tamar of Galilee

Rabbi Cohn opened the door to the conference room down the hall from the sanctuary and next to his office. The room had a long table that could easily seat twelve to fifteen people. One of the mostly bare walls hosted a large, seventy-five-inch TV at one end. "Please take a seat, everyone," he instructed.

Everyone proceeded to sit except for a young man in his early thirties or so. He turned on the TV, then went to the back of the room, where he began setting up various technical devices and some electrical equipment.

"Allow me to introduce you, Tamar," said Rabbi Cohn, gesturing toward each person in turn. "You already know the Abrams family. This is Jonathan Rosen, our resident historian and main presenter for today's meeting. The gentleman handling all of our technical needs is Bob Edwards. And last but certainly not least, my lovely wife, Elizabeth Cohn."

Elizabeth stood and turned to face Tamar. She asked politely, "Is it okay if I hug you? I've always been a hugger." Tamar smiled warmly and stood to embrace the kind-hearted woman.

"Brother Jonathan, will you please hand me the scrolls?" the rabbi requested.

"Yes, Rabbi," Jonathan promptly responded.

Rabbi Cohn began addressing Tamar. "First and foremost, we thank God for all He has done in your life. We are in awe of how you were lost and now have been found. Your journey to this point is beyond our understanding, but we are grateful for the opportunity to witness it today." Those seated around the table nodded in agreement. "Today, you will meet the other two. You have already met and talked to Tony, but today, you will also meet Rayford Witt."

Tamar interrupted, "They are coming here?"

"No, they'll be joining us by phone on a conference call." Bob gave the rabbi a thumbs up to indicate everything was ready, and Rabbi Cohn continued. "It would be better to explain everything to all three of you at once," he explained. "Go ahead, Bob, set it up."

The big screen flickered before two black screens appeared in the center. Bob clicked the Join Now button on the left screen and Tony quickly appeared.

"We can see you, Mr. Hall," said Bob. "Try unmuting your mic."

The red symbol over the microphone disappeared and Tony asked, "Can you hear me?"

"Yes, we can hear you clearly, sir," Bob replied as he clicked the invite icon on the other quadrant. Ray suddenly appeared, and the sight of him moved Tamar to tears, though her intense focus made her oblivious to the salty tracks running down her cheeks.

"Hello, everyone," Ray said, looking at each person in the room. They acknowledged his greeting with nods and smiles.

Rabbi Cohn spoke up. "Welcome, gentlemen. We are honored to have you join us on this momentous occasion."

He proceeded to introduce each person in the room until he reached Tamar. "And this is our special guest, Tanya Bloom. We may refer to her as 'Tamar,' because she has been linked with an important part of her past which you will soon witness. I know you all must have questions, so please write them down and we will try to address them at the end. Now, I'd like to turn it over to our historian, Elder Jonathan Rosen, to begin our discussion. Please proceed, brother . . ." The rabbi gestured toward Jonathan.

"First and foremost, you all should know that we are all Levitical Jews," Brother Rosen began, then Bob cleared his throat. "Oh, sorry Bob," he chuckled. "Except for Bob. He is the embodiment of a red, white, and true-blue American." The Rabbi and Mrs. Cohn snickered at the remark.

"However," Rosen continued, "we are also Messianic Jews. We believe in the life, death, and resurrection of Christ, who is seated at the right hand of the Father." Everyone nodded in agreement at this fundamental truth.

"As Levites and Essenes, we have always been viewed as outcasts and have often operated in the shadows of mainstream Judaism. But as with the Dead Sea Scrolls, we have preserved our history through meticulous documentation. Our community has long been aware of your existence, but not until 150 years ago did we actively begin searching for you three. Before we continue, I want to clarify why we didn't simply have all of you gather at the church," Rosen began, carefully pulling out an old scroll, copied over centuries by scribes, and laying it out on the table.

"This isn't the original scroll, but it contains the thoughts and beliefs of prominent figures such as Polycarp, Clement, Caius, Augustine, and Jerome. They were, of course, the Apostolic Fathers who gave special witness to our faith, some dying the death of martyrs," Rosen continued. "It has become known as the Essenes' Mishnah, or the written collection of their oral contributions to the faith."

"Brother, I think they understand," Rabbi Cohn interjected. "Remember, all of our guests have a unique perspective on history, perhaps even relationships with these spiritual fathers."

"My apologies, everyone. I am very passionate about history and could go on for days. But right here," Rosen pointed to a specific section on the scroll, "the Fathers all agree that there is a designated time and place for all of you to meet face-to-face. It's written very clearly."

"What is written clearly?" Tony interrupted.

"Please, let him finish," Ray asserted calmly, but with authority.

"Apologies," Tony replied.

Rabbi Cohn joined in. "We are very certain that you three are to return to Jerusalem. God has appointed a time and place, according to this scroll, where you three should encounter Him."

Rosen added, "This is a very special place on earth. Millennium after millennium, God shows up here, as prophesied in this scroll. It actually bears the name of God."

"Where is it?" Tamar inquired.

"That's a great question," Rosen replied. "It's called 'Ha-Makom,' or literally, 'the place.' It's where our father Abraham offered up Isaac. In many Jewish sects, it's known as 'YHVH Yireh,' a very sacred and holy name.

Tony unmuted his microphone and asked flawlessly in Yiddish, "What does 'YHVH Yireh' mean?"

"Sir, that is the question of the day, and it's crucial to your understanding," Rosen stated with conviction. "It can have various interpretations, but it also could ultimately convey one important message. 'Yireh' means to manifest, present oneself, to provide, to become visible, even to reveal. As seen in Abraham's case, God manifested himself and intervened to prevent Abraham from sacrificing Isaac, but He also provided a ram in the bush."

Ray raised an eyebrow and challenged, "So, you think that if we all gather at 'the place,' God will make an appearance and reveal something to us?"

"Exactly," replied the rabbi. "And not only that, but this is also the exact place the second Moses visited, traveled to, and ultimately died in."

"Jesus," Tamar interjected with excitement. "I understand. Jesus came as a sacrificial offering, like the ram caught in the bushes for Abraham and Isaac. So, according to the scroll, if we return to 'the place,' God may once again choose to reveal Himself to us in a fuller way?"

"Precisely," Rosen explained. "We have faith that He will provide something for each of you. What exactly, we cannot say for certain."

"Where is this place?" Tony inquired.

"Mount Moriah!" Ray replied with perfect cadence. "Where Abraham bound Isaac for sacrifice, and where Solomon built the Temple. Geographically, it's also where Jacob dreamed of a ladder that connected us to heaven, but more than anything, where our true bridge to God, Jesus, was crucified."

Everyone took a moment to process the significance of his insight. "Father Abraham, Jacob, Jesus and now us?" Tanya wondered aloud. "That is some pretty serious company!"

"So, when are we supposed to go to this 'place'?" Tony asked.

"Well—" Rosen began.

"We believe it should be sometime this year during Yovel, the Jubilee," Elizabeth interjected.

"Yes," Rosen confirmed. "This marks the fifty-year period when God will supernaturally liberate, restore, and release His power over Israel, all those who belong to Him in Spirit and in truth."

"Yovel literally means 'year of liberty, freedom, and victory,'" Rabbi Cohn explained. "It signifies a time of restoration."

"And when does this Yovel take place?" Tamar inquired.

"In October of this year," the rabbi replied. "According to Leviticus 25, it falls on the tenth day of the month of Tishrei, the first month of our Jewish year."

Tamar frowned, her brow furrowed with worry. "It's already August. And we're supposed to be in Israel by October?"

The rabbi nodded solemnly. "Yes, and if the three of you abandon the Lord's beckoning call for the designated time, you'll continue wandering the earth, yet in barrenness of life, short of all He has for you."

A tense silence fell. "I'm not sure about all this," Ray said, voicing everyone's hesitation. "After my recent experiences in the Middle East, I'm not exactly eager to go back. How do you know for certain?"

Tony unmuted and added his concerns. "I don't have vacation time left for a trip like that. This will upend my life over what seems a bit like speculation, based on ancient documents." Tamar simply nodded in agreement with their sentiments.

Unexpectedly, a soft knock sounded at the door. Bob cautiously opened it, and a boy peeked his head in. "It's your time!" he announced, then pulled back and disappeared from view.

Tamar rushed toward the door. "I know that boy!" She flung the door open and scanned the long hallway, sitting empty and silent. Left, right, she saw no one. She sprinted toward the nearest exit, but there was no one in sight. She returned to the conference room.

Tony was baffled. "What just happened? Who was that kid?"

"He vanished, but I know him!" Tanya replied.

Bob's eyes widened. "Wait a minute. There one moment and gone the next? And you guys saw him too?" he asked Ray and Tony, incredulous.

"Of course we did," they confirmed in unison.

"But it makes no sense," Bob argued, gesturing to the camera angle. "You both should clearly see everyone at the table, but the door is not in the frame. It would be impossible for you to see the door or anyone in it from the current camera angle." Everyone exchanged glances in search of an explanation.

"Can someone please explain who that kid was?" Tony demanded, frustrated.

Tanya spoke up. "He was with me on the day of my accident. He brought me a magazine with a picture of you, Ray. The police tried to talk to him, but he ran off and disappeared into the crowd."

Ray joined in. "I've seen that kid before too. He came to our apartment a while ago selling candy for some trip to the Holy Land. But I don't think he was there to sell us candy. Something inexplicable happened when my wife Monica and I touched his hand together. We had been arguing, but when he touched us, all the tension dissipated. Then he disappeared down the steps. We were left at the door, holding hands."

"How is it possible he was with both of you when you needed help," Tony questioned, "that this same boy was with you, Tanya, during the accident and with you, Ray, when you needed help, and here now, at this crucial moment for us?"

Rabbi Cohn turned to address the group calmly. "You should have no doubt. *It's your time!*"

CHAPTER TWENTY EIGHT

It Ain't Easy

Tony sat in his man cave long after the meeting ended, thinking through everything that had occurred. So many events defied all natural explanation. It was mind-boggling: most recently the boy who appeared at their door, challenging logic but also the laws of time and space. Tony was a walking, talking miracle, but he never quite got used to that either.

How could he break the news to Julie, that he had to leave for Israel in less than a month? She was already upset about all the recent secrecy, including the private internet meeting he had attended. She knew him well enough to know this behavior wasn't normal.

Sitting in his executive chair, he leaned back and closed his eyes. He cried out to God, desperate for help. "Throughout my life, I've always tried to handle things on my own, my way. But this time, I can't do it alone." He thought of his beloved wife, and the weight of the situation hit him hard. "This is bigger than me; it's bigger than all of us. God, I surrender my own desires. Please show me the way. Guide me through this difficult time."

His eyes fluttered open and he saw Julie standing next to him, tears cascading down her cheeks. He sat up quickly in his chair, nearly tipping it over from shock. Julie dropped to her knees beside him and buried her head in his lap, crying. Tony tenderly stroked her red hair without saying a word. "I'll go wherever you go," she managed, as they sat in quiet unity.

Across town, after Ray had also logged off from the meeting, Monica gave him a knowing look. "Well, that was certainly revealing."

Ray leaned in closer to her. "You saw the boy, too, right honey?"

"Yes, I saw him. And yes, he's the same boy who came to our door."

"What do you think about all this?"

"I feel just as involved in this as you," Monica replied. "I'm the one who submitted your DNA and went to the Abrams' house. You can count on me to support you through all of it, no matter where it leads."

"Thanks, babe. I'm so grateful for that. I never doubted your loyalty."

"But let's remember, no one said this would be easy."

CHAPTER TWENTY NINE

Goodbyes

This restaurant is way fancier than I'm used to, RJ thought as he fidgeted with his tie.

"I'm meeting someone," he informed the hostess, scanning the room. He saw Tanya at a distance, but he had never seen her like that! Her hair fell over her shoulders, and a sparkling dress accentuated her figure.

"What's up?" Tanya asked when RJ arrived at the table.

"You!" he replied without hesitation. Tanya blushed as her co-worker sat across from her.

"You clean up pretty nice too," Tanya added to break the ice.

"Thanks, Tanya," RJ replied sincerely. "So, I can have anything I want, huh?" RJ asked in unbelief.

"Yes," Tanya affirmed.

"Man, this must be something important."

"It is," Tanya said with emotion.

Small talk mixed in with their normal banter occupied the next half hour. "This was a good meal," RJ commented, tossing his napkin on the table, "but my boys at Ramsey's Chicken Hut could have hooked us up for half of what this cost." His comment would have surely set off conflict a few months earlier. But this was a new Tanya, changed by recent events, and she wasn't about to go back to her old ways.

"RJ, I'm taking some time away from the job, and I may not be back."

"What, are you serious?" he asked incredulously. "You're gonna to leave me after all these years? I'm just getting used to you. Now you're gonna bounce on me? Why, Tanya?" he pleaded.

"Would you like to see a dessert menu?" a waitress asked.

"No!" RJ answered rudely, catching her off guard.

"Maybe a little later," Tanya said calmly. "We'll let you know."

"Very well then, ma'am," she responded, walking away with the dishes.

"RJ, I have had some major changes in my life recently."

"You mean like getting hit by a truck?" RJ interrupted.

"Yes, that and much more. I think I've found some long lost relatives and other people who are like me in some important ways."

"Yeah, but—" RJ interjected.

"RJ, just let me finish, please. I have reconnected with my roots, and my journey is taking me back to Israel and my Jewish heritage. I've rededicated my life to God, and I am changed. I'm flying out in a few days to Jerusalem, and I have no idea what will happen there, but I must go."

"So, you done gone religious on me now? You saw God when that truck hit you just like in the movies?"

"Yes, something like that my friend, something like that."

Carrie was already in her pajamas curled up on the couch when Tanya arrived home from dinner. "What's happening, roomie, and why are you looking all dapper?"

"Oh, I took RJ out to eat at a nice restaurant. We needed to talk."

"About what?" inquired Carrie.

"Actually, I want to talk to you, too, but I want to get comfortable first, is that cool?"

"Sure!" Carrie replied.

Tanya went into her room and within minutes had neatly hung her dress clothes and stored her shoes in their proper place. She quickly washed off the little make-up she thought necessary for the evening out. She looked in the mirror and a strange sensation washed over her. *If anyone is in Christ, he is a new creation. The old has passed away; behold, the new has come.*[10]

"Did I say that, or did I hear it?" She looked more intently in the mirror and heard it again. It was her voice, but her lips hadn't moved. *You are ready*, came a voice from her spirit, and she knew exactly what that meant.

Returning to the couch, Tanya sat next to her best friend and grabbed her hand. She repeated the goodbye she had said earlier to RJ, while Carrie sat in silence. "My friend, God has had so much grace and mercy on me my whole life, and I want you to experience that too. I know you've noticed some changes in me lately."

"True. You are so calm, and you have a peace about you, a radiant glow like a woman waiting to give birth. I don't know. I can't explain it," Carrie continued.

"It's Christ in me," Tanya said matter-of-factly. "Before I leave, I want to give you the same opportunity I gave RJ earlier tonight. Although his heart wasn't ready, I know yours is. First and foremost, God loves you so much and He is ready with the gift of everlasting life, just for you. Are you ready to receive it?" she asked.

"Yes, I'm ready," came Carrie's still, small voice.

Okay, my dearest friend, repeat this after me: Dear God, I know I'm a sinner, and I ask for your forgiveness. I believe Jesus Christ is Your Son, that he died on the cross for my sins and rose again to life. I believe that in my

---

[10] 1 Corinthians 5:16 RSV

heart and I confess with my mouth, that Jesus is my Savior and Lord. Thank You for saving me, in Jesus' name I pray, amen.

Some goodbyes are not goodbyes at all, Tanya thought.

CHAPTER THIRTY

Jerusalem

Tanya arrived first in Israel, followed by Tony and Julie, then Ray and Monica. Everyone made it through the Ben Gurion Airport in Tel Aviv on time and without incident. Ray and Monica passed through customs, where they quickly spotted their names on a sign. Ray extended his hand to the man holding the sign.

"Hello, I'm Ray Witt," he introduced himself. The man eagerly shook his hand.

"I'm Adam Shulman, and this is my wife, Abigail. We are your hosts. It's a pleasure to meet you."

Ray gestured. "This is my wife, Monica."

After a brief walk, they retrieved their luggage and stepped out of the terminal. A white minivan waited for them, and a young man in his twenties quickly loaded all their bags into the back compartment.

"This is our son, Micah," Abigail introduced him. "Pleasure to meet you," the Witts said in unison, entering the van.

As they exited the airport, armed military guards halted their vehicle. "ID, please," one asked Micah, while the other inspected the van. After completing a full circle around it, he whispered something to his colleague in charge, then returned to the driver's window.

"We need to see everyone's passport and ID," he demanded. The three family members in the car quickly presented their cards while Ray and Monica rummaged through their backpacks for their passports. Micah handed all the documents to the guard, who scrutinized them carefully. After a moment, he seemed satisfied and waved the van through. The other guard had already moved on to inspect the next vehicle.

"Is this normal?" Ray asked, addressing no one in particular.

"Yes, it's just part of life in Israel," Adam replied.

The van slowly navigated through Tel Aviv traffic as it headed toward Route 443 to Jerusalem, about a forty-minute drive through rolling hills and mountains, with small talk filling the time.

"You'll be staying in our home," Abigail said from the front passenger seat. "We should arrive in time for a light meal before calling it a night. Hopefully you're tired enough to get some rest."

Monica admitted, "I don't think that will be an issue. I'm completely drained from the flight."

"Sleep is nearly impossible for me on planes," Ray added.

As the group reached the summit of the mountain at Mevaseret Zion, a town about six miles west of Jerusalem, the stunning panoramic sight of Jerusalem below greeted them. The bright lights with the old city standing out in all its splendor captivated them. Monica asked, "What's that illuminated part of the city, with the military personnel guarding it?"

The Shulmans responded in unison, "That is the Western Wall."

Monica sat in awe as she leaned over Ray to see the structure rushing past them.

Ray reminisced about the times he had spent admiring it, worshipping God, and hanging out with friends at the Wailing Wall. It wasn't too far from his hometown, Bethlehem, a place in a time that seemed so much simpler. Fatigue weighed on him. *Wonder if I'll even make it back there . . . It's only nine kilometers away.* Before long, they arrived at a modest home in the heart of Jerusalem.

Two young girls, about nine years old, rushed through the door and latched onto their mother's waist. "Ima, Ima,"[11] they both exclaimed, trying to outdo each other for attention.

"Shira and Sarah, be quiet please. Where is Doda Isabella?"[12] their mother scolded.

The taller of the two girls replied, "She's in the kitchen, Mama."

---

[11] Ima means "Mommy" in Hebrew, signifying the matriarch of the family and fundamental source of life, as established by God.
[12] Doda, in Hebrew, means "aunt."

"Monica and Ray, these are our twins, Shira and Sarah," Adam introduced them.

Monica greeted them warmly while Shira blurted out, "I am older."

"But only by ten minutes!" Sarah added.

"Girls, let Mr. and Mrs. Witt come in; they are exhausted from their trip," Adam said firmly. He then led the couple to their room at the back of the house.

Later, as everyone gathered around the table, Monica reflected on the scene. *This seems so similar, like a typical American household.* Auntie Isabella served the skillfully prepared traditional meal of roasted chicken, matzo balls, and several potato dishes.

Ray and Monica enjoyed the home-cooked meal and pleasant conversation, but jet lag weighed heavily on them and they were ready to call it a night. Monica spoke first, excusing herself. "Thank you for the wonderful meal. I'm ready to sleep! Have a good night, everyone."

"Yeah, goodnight, and thanks for your hospitality," Ray agreed.

The next morning, when they made their way down to the dining table, the entire family was already seated. Shira and Sarah eagerly looked over at Ray, curious to finally meet this man they had heard so much about. Shira couldn't hold back her question any longer. "Dad," she said, leaning forward, "is this the man from Bethlehem you were searching for? He looks like any other man to me."

"Shh!" scolded their mother. "You can't ask those types of questions."

"Why not?" Sarah chimed in. "We've been hearing about him our whole life, and now he's here at our table. Why can't we talk to him?"

"Grow up!" Micah said without looking up from his *bourekas*[13] and coffee.

"That's enough, girls!" their father intervened sternly. "Micah, you should know better too."

Micah simply shrugged his shoulders without looking up from his plate.

Adam grumbled before changing the subject. "After we finish eating, let's move into the living room." Ray nodded in agreement.

As everyone settled in the living room, Adam began the conversation. "Ray, today we will take you to our temple to meet Rabbi Aaronson. Our appointment is at 1:00 p.m. We suggest that you go alone. My wife can take Monica around to see some of our most famous sites and shop.

"I have no secrets from Monica," Ray blurted out before realizing how absurd that sounded. Everyone in the room looked at him incredulously before Monica broke the awkward silence.

"It's fine, Ray. I have some things I'd like to see."

---

[13] Bourekas are common turnover pastries in Israeli cuisine, often stuffed with various savory fillings.

Ray realized just how much he had relied on Monica. She was his rock, and he couldn't imagine going through this journey without her by his side. "Okay, babe."

Later that day, Ray and Adam arrived at the temple's parking lot, close to 1:00. The room was already bustling with people.

Rabbi Cohn was the first to welcome Ray and Adam. "How was your flight from New York?" he asked.

"It was a lengthy journey, without much sleep, but I'll be alright," Ray responded.

A traditional Jewish man, tall and lean, dressed in a kippah, tallit,[14] and kittel,[15] approached the group. To Ray's amazement, he even had side curls peeking out from under his headwear.

Rabbi Cohn spoke up. "This is Rabbi Aaronson; he will be leading today's meeting."

"Shabbat Shalom, Ray. It's an honor to meet you. Please have a seat," Rabbi Aaronson offered as he gestured toward a chair. Ray greeted the rabbi and the others in the room.

"I'll keep the introductions brief," Rabbi Aaronson assured everyone. "You already know some of the people here, such as Rabbi Cohn, Dr. and Mr.

---

[14] A tallit is a prayer shawl, typically white with fringes at the four corners, worn over the head and shoulders by Jewish men for religious purposes.
[15] A kittel is a white robe worn by orthodox Jewish men (and sometimes women) on Yom Kippur, Rosh Hashanah, and at the Passover Seder.

Abrams, and Adam, but everyone in this room has been instrumental in locating you. We have our wise men or historians (*hakham*), who are proficient in the Torah; rabbis and other experts on the Talmud, a central text for our Jewish tradition, teaching, and law; as well as devout leaders from the Essenes sect. Most importantly, we are all Messianic Jews, holding that the New Testament is an essential part of the entire biblical canon. Do you have any questions about that, Ray?"

"I don't believe so, Rabbi," Ray answered.

"Very well then, I will continue. Two days ago, we met with Tamar since she arrived first, and we spoke with Tony this morning. So now, it's just you! We are thrilled to welcome you home!"

"Thank you all for the hospitality you have shown my wife and me. It is much more than we could have asked for," Ray continued. "It's our hope that we can get answers to some of our questions!"

"That is the hope for all of us," Rabbi Cohn responded, then pointed to a gentleman across the table. "That man is our Kohen,[16] Rabbi Katz. He leads a team of other rabbis, *gabbais, rebbes, and tzaddikim.* Are you familiar with those ecclesiastical positions?" Rabbi Aaronson asked.

"Very," Ray said without hesitation. "A Kohen is an Aaronic priest, gabbais are synagogue overseers, rebbes are teachers, and tzaddikim are judges," Ray added, pointing in the direction of each man.

Rabbi Cohn commended his knowledge. "Excellent. Then, we can move on to why we are all here."

---

[16] Kohen: A descendent of Moses' brother, Aaron (from the biblical book of Genesis).

All heads in the room nodded in affirmation.

Rabbi Aaronson's voice filled the small synagogue hall. "This is the year of Yovel, also known as the Jubilee. For half a century, we have been waiting for this time of liberation, freedom, and triumph. It's a time when our people reclaim our inheritance and regain all that has been lost to us. We just finished celebrating Rosh Hashanah, a fresh start in the Jewish new year, and today we are eight days in to the ten Days of Repentance (or Days of Awe), ending with Yom Kippur, the Day of Atonement. We believe on that day God has something special in store for you and for us. It has been our fervent prayer to find you three before this Jubilee cycle ends. The individuals gathered here have worked diligently for the past fifty years, spanning three generations before us. Do you understand the significance of everything, man from Bethlehem?" The rabbi inquired with curiosity.

"Yes, I do," replied Ray. "I believe I know where we need to be: on Mount Moriah. But I don't understand the reason why, what you expect to happen there."

"Those are excellent questions," responded the Rabbi. "We anticipate a special blessing from God in two days, on Yom Kippur, unlike anything that has happened in history. On that day, our entire community worldwide will be reading from our Holy Prayer Book, the Machzor.

"With Yovel, Rash Hashanah, and Yom Kippur all occurring in the first month of Tishrei, it is crucial you three are together in one place. It is then that YHVH Yireh, God, will move in a miraculous way!" exclaimed the Rabbi with excitement.

"And do what?" Ray inquired.

"That, my son, is unknown to us," answered Rabbi Cohn. "It is a mystery, but we know He has always been faithful to us, and He has done great and mighty things during many High and Holy Days. We believe He will do it again on this day."

A shofar blast echoed throughout the chamber and sent shockwaves through the room. Every person in the room broke out in spontaneous worship at the unexpected sound. Voices rose, praising God in all different languages— in Hebrew, Yiddish, and English, while others spoke in tongues. Rabbis Aaronson and Cohn, overcome by a sudden rush of wind, dropped to their knees, praying and worshiping God. His mighty power moved throughout the room, and tears streamed down Ray's face as God touched him. He fell flat on the floor, just like the day in his closet, completely overcome by the Spirit of God.

It was so good to be home!

CHAPTER THIRTY ONE

Bound in Glory
(Part 1)

The next evening, Monica and Ray held hands as they strolled through a park near Rabbi Aaronson's house. Monica couldn't shake the strange mix of emotions swirling inside her. She felt excitement in the Holy Land, yet an unidentifiable dread and sadness, that something terrible was about to happen. She turned to Ray, searching for answers. "What am I missing? Your past has always been a mystery to me, and I've respected your desire for privacy. Yet here I am in Israel, chasing after something unknown. I'm at my breaking point!"

Ray sat down on a nearby bench and gazed deeply into her eyes. "I wish I had all the answers, but I strongly believe something significant will happen tomorrow," he replied. "My whole life seems to be leading up to this moment."

"Something significant with you? What's going on? What is that supposed to mean?"

Ray took a deep breath before responding. "Yes, with me. And quite possibly with Tony and Tanya too."

"Ray, you can't keep hiding things from me. Ever since the DNA testing, something has been really off, with more riddles than usual. Way more. Please," she implored, tell me the truth!"

"Let's just enjoy tonight, babe. Tomorrow, everything will be revealed," he said with a rare quietness and uncertainty in his voice. Monica hardly recognized him—quiet, hesitant, and unsure of himself. He had changed drastically.

She relented. "Okay, let's spend some quality time together, as if it's our last."

"Monica, do you remember what I told you on our wedding day?"

"Not word for word."

Ray reached into the vest pocket of his jacket and pulled out an envelope with a piece of paper in it, neatly folded and obviously cared for. He began to read:

> *Today I am filled with an overwhelming sense of gratitude and love, because I am marrying my best friend. You are my rock, my confidante, and aside from God, my greatest blessing. I love you wholeheartedly, and my love knows no bounds. Once our time on earth is finished, even then will I still love you. My love, Monica, I have no doubt we will find and hold each other again, for all eternity.*

Ray carefully folded the paper and returned it to its envelope before handing it to her, overcome with emotion.

Not far away, Tony and Julie were strolling through Jerusalem Metropolitan Park, a vibrant garden, having a similar discussion. Julie gently stopped Tony, her arm in his, to share her heart. "Tony, I have a bad feeling about this trip. Why are we here?" she asked, feeling sick to her stomach.

"I don't have all the answers, Jules. But that's a valid question," he replied, knowing he couldn't keep the truth hidden forever. I am not who you think I am, but at the same time, I am exactly who you think I am," he confessed.

"What does that even mean?" she asked, confused and frustrated. "Are you some sort of devoted husband by day and secret agent by night? Are you an alien from another planet?"

"No, nothing like that," he reassured her.

"Well, then who are you?" she demanded.

"Darling, I believe everything will be laid bare tomorrow. I just want to enjoy a peaceful evening together, to enjoy us." He reached out to comfort her, but two doves interrupted his motion, flying past them and perching on a nearby tree. They watched the birds coo into the quiet night.

"Do you think that's a coincidence?" she asked, pointing toward the doves. "The Bible says doves are birds of peace. Is God speaking to us?"

"A coincidence?" Tony remarked. "No, I don't believe so." He wrapped his arms around her. "I think the days of chance occurrences are behind us."

Each couple embraced in a separate paradise, basking in the moonlit night over Jerusalem, the Eternal City of God.

CHAPTER THIRTY TWO

Bound in Glory
(Part 2)

The next morning, Rabbi Aaronson brought Tony and Julie to The Church of the Holy Sepulcher, the holiest site of Christianity, believed to be the location of Jesus' death, burial, and resurrection. Rabbi Cohn accompanied Ray and Monica, while Alexandra and Benjamin escorted Tanya. Each party was led to separate areas near the sepulcher, the burial site of Jesus.

Tanya listened as beautiful prayer melodies resonated from the sanctuary chamber, sounding like choirs of angels. "Who is singing and praying in there?" she asked out of curiosity.

"Our people from all over Israel and the world," Alexandra replied.

"Messianic Jews?" Tanya clarified.

"Yes, that's right," she confirmed. "Please put on this white gown and tallit," she requested, handing Tanya the garments.

"It's been a while since I wore one of these," Tanya remarked as she slid the gown over her head.

"Let me help you with this tichel," Alexandra added, moving behind her to help with the head covering. A stranger entered the room and whispered something in her ear.

"Okay," she said. "We're almost ready."

"For what?" Tanya questioned.

"To go into the sanctuary. Tony and Ray are getting dressed in their rooms and will be ready soon."

The rabbis assisted Tony and Ray, outfitting them in traditional Jewish attire: kippahs; tallits; and tefillin, small boxes carrying the Shema—the core belief of Judaism and Christianity—to love God with every part of their being. Both men stood with their wives by their side. Mixed emotions filled them all—wonder, worry, confusion, anticipation—as they prepared for a ceremony unlike any they had experienced before.

"Let's go," Rabbi Cohn instructed Ray. "My wife will take Monica to her place."

Ray turned to Monica, "Come here, beautiful." They shared a powerful yet tender embrace and a kiss before entering into the unknown. As Monica walked away, she felt the weight of this pivotal moment; tears threatened to fall from her eyes.

In the adjacent room, Tony and Julie said their goodbyes. "Please reconsider this," Julie urged. "We don't know these people, and we are so far from home," she pleaded, desperately grasping for reasons why he should stay.

"We've come so far," he said, trying to calm her. "Something incredible is going to happen today. I just know it. With God's help, we can do this, Jules! I need your support, no matter what happens. Can you give that?"

"I think so." Her tears flowed freely.

Rabbi Aaronson approached them, taking their hands in his own. "Lord God, help us all to be strong. Today more than ever, we don't lean on our own understanding; we turn everything over to You. Our God, please be a very present help to Tony and Julie right here, right now. They need You. Place Your joy and Shalom peace in their hearts. Do this, Lord, all for your glory. Amen."

With that, they left the room.

Rabbi Aaronson entered the sanctuary, walking to the front to address the congregation. "Today is a momentous day, one that our ancestors have prayed for, for over a millennium. We haven't felt this much joy since 1947, when the world first discovered our sacred writings in the caves of Qumran. Even more, we remember and honor one of our own, John the Baptizer, who prepared the way for our Messiah, Jesus, over two thousand years ago, that both Jews and Gentiles alike might recognize and know Him as the Savior of the world. Now, we have reason to rejoice over 'the lost three,' gathered today in this holy place."

His words echoed throughout the space, filling Monica with awe. For the first time, she truly noticed the magnificent church. Her earlier focus on their mission had eclipsed her ability to appreciate the surroundings.

Looking behind her, Monica saw the Rock of Golgotha, the site of Jesus' crucifixion, now marked by a cross. Turning forward again and looking up, she gasped at the beautiful golden-and-blue dome above the sanctuary. She gazed up once more, following the beam of light shining down onto the marble slab, where tradition claims Jesus' body lay in the tomb before He rose from the dead. The beauty and significance of this sacred place overwhelmed her.

She tuned in again to Rabbi Aaronson's words, as he motioned toward three rabbis, each standing in front of a different chamber door, where the three exited. One by one, they led Tanya, Tony, and Ray out of the chamber and onto three elevated platforms facing the front of the sanctuary.

"On my left stands Tanya, Tamar of Galilee, and on my right is Tony of Nain. And directly in front of me is Ray, the man from Bethlehem." The rabbi gestured to each person in turn. "Our ancient writings and scrolls instructed us to bring these three here, to the place our Savior was laid to rest," he said, motioning toward a nearby chamber. "Here, where the angel rolled away the stone, because Jesus had risen from the dead." The room fell silent as they considered the eternal significance for all humanity of this place, of the events that had occurred here.

"My fellow believers, we have gathered with hopeful hearts, but none of us know what comes next. There is no road map, no guidance moving forward. Let us seek God's heart for today."

A voice from the crowd pierced the silence. "Please, have them introduce themselves."

"Who said that?" Rabbi Aaronson asked, curious.

"I did," a boy answered as he emerged from the crowd. He walked past Ray and stood in front of Rabbi Aaronson. "Have them start from the beginning of their lives, and tell us who they are," he repeated with authority.

"Well, I suppose we could do that," Rabbi Aaronson stuttered. The boy turned toward the three.

"It's him!" Tanya exclaimed, pointing. "The boy from the accident!"

"Wait a minute!" Tony interjected. "He's the boy from our video conference. He said, 'It's your time,' then ran away."

"Oh, my Jesus," Ray exclaimed, "and he visited our apartment, when we needed help. He's been with all of us in recent months!"

The boy turned to the crowd. "I am not the focal point here." He turned to Tony. "Please, tell everyone who you are."

As Tony gazed at the boy, he noticed a peculiar radiance on his face, both comforting and calming, filling him with peace as he began to speak. "I grew up in a small village near Nazareth with only my mother. My father had passed away years earlier, so I worked hard to provide for my family. One day, I fell ill and was unable to work. My mother sought medical help for me, yet my condition did not improve. I don't remember much after that, except longing for relief from the fever and chills consuming me."

Tony paused to catch his breath. "My memory fades after that, except I soon found myself in a chamber with complete silence, and bright, illuminating light. It was peaceful in a way I had never felt, nor could I possibly explain—as if I were not alive, yet not dead either. Just peacefully existing.

"I was told that I died," Tony shared sadly. "My mother said months later that she and the townspeople had mourned my passing for three days. She was heartbroken. On the day of my burial, following our tradition for mourners, my friends and family were weeping loudly when a man approached us. My silent body lay resting on a funeral bier. He spoke words of comfort and compassion to her, and from that quiet resting place, I heard His thunderous voice command, *Asher, arise!*'

"In the blink of an eye, I left the place of rest and entered my body, which was lying in a coffin. I awoke, sat straight up, and wondered aloud, 'Where am I? What's happening?' The man simply replied, 'Shalom, to you and your mother.' Then he walked away."

With those final words, Tony's demeanor suddenly changed. His face seemed to shine and his hair stood on end, as if a strong wind held it midair. He threw his arms straight out and upward to heaven. In a focused and full state of joy, eyes fixed on the boy, he declared, "*I am Asher of Naim!*"

Awe filled the room. Sorrow and wonder pervaded Julie's heart as she watched and listened to her husband; at least, the man she believed was her husband. She longed to go to him and embrace him, her natural mind in a quandary, but in her soul, she knew to stay seated and still. The comforting hand of Mrs. Aaronson covered hers. They squeezed hands, bracing for what would come next.

Everyone's gaze turned back to the boy, glowing with a magnificent aura. He transformed into a confident and mature young man. Monica saw the light shining from the dome shift to engulf him.

With a commanding tone, he pointed directly at Tanya and spoke with unwavering authority. "Tell everyone who you are!" Tanya filled with joy and calmness. She had waited for what seemed an eternity to share her story with someone, anyone, who would truly listen.

"Shortly after I was born, I contracted tuberculosis. My father was a very wealthy and powerful man who held a position of authority in the local temple. When I reached the age of twelve, I fell deathly ill from the disease. My chest ached constantly and I coughed uncontrollably. I became weaker and more fatigued with each passing day, until I could no longer leave my bed.

"My parents loved me very much and never left my side. Or at least, that's what I thought. I later discovered that my father did leave me. He had heard of a man who could heal the sick; He even raised people from the dead. So, he set out to find Him.

"Several days later, my father found himself in a large crowd of people, all trying to catch a glimpse of the man from Galilee, Jesus. He searched through the throng until he finally found Him. He quickly fell to his knees, begging Him to come and heal me. To my father's great relief, He agreed.

"As people pushed and shoved their way through the tightly packed crowd, the man stopped and asked, 'Who touched me?' My father was confused. How could anyone possibly know who had touched him with so many people pressing against him on all sides? But the man asked again, causing one of the men traveling with him to voice what everyone was thinking: that all sorts of people were touching him as they struggled to get close.

"The crowd parted to reveal a woman known in the region as Dinah, frail and unclean. By Jewish Law, she could touch no one. She often looked pale and sickly, with sunken eyes and a gaunt frame. She timidly claimed, 'I did,' then collapsed from exhaustion or perhaps fright—my father couldn't tell.

"The man turned and walked back to her. He reached down and helped her up, pulling her close. He whispered, 'Daughter, your faith has made you whole.' My father saw the miraculous transformation before his very eyes. The woman's once pale skin turned rosy and full of life, while her dull and lonely eyes began to fill and dance with joy. She stood before the crowd, whole, healed, and beautiful, her sickly appearance replaced with heavenly grace.

"My father witnessed everything. After seeing this amazing miracle unfold before his very eyes, it filled him with even greater hope that Jesus could certainly heal me. Then, Mattias, one of our loyal servants, hesitantly broke the news to him: I had succumbed to the disease. It crushed my father's optimism.

"His tears fell to the ground in the same spot where the frail and broken woman had just been cured. The teacher knelt down and offered a hand to help my beloved father up, whispering something to him as they slowly made their way to our home.

"To be honest, I don't recall anything besides falling into a deep slumber. No bright lights, dreams, or disruptions, just peaceful sleep. Time seemed to stand still, to never end. My emotions were neither joyful nor sorrowful, I simply remained in a state of calm.

"When my father and his fellow travelers arrived, they found our household deep in mourning over my passing. The Aninut stage of mourning, between death and burial, had begun, with everyone fully immersed in the grieving process.

My father spoke up. "Jesus has commanded everyone to stop crying, especially the town mourners." This Rabbi, Jesus, then told everyone that I was simply sleeping, not dead! This caused quite a bit of confusion, as my death had already been confirmed. My handmaid and lifelong best friend, Simone, later recounted how she had held my cold body for an hour before being forced to let go.

"At the Rabbi's instruction, He walked into my room with just my mother, father, and three other men. Years later, I would become acquainted with these three individuals on a personal level. They confirmed I was legally deceased before the Teacher's arrival.

"I couldn't fathom how this had happened, but as I rested in that peaceful chamber, I felt a hand gently grasp mine, and I heard the Teacher's voice command me, *"Maiden, arise."* I remember it as clearly as if he were standing before me now. He didn't pull me out of the chamber, he simply touched me and spoke those words. When I finally opened my eyes, my spirit had re-entered my body in my bed, as if I had just woken up from a normal night's rest. The scent of incense and burial herbs filled the air, but the gentle touch of my mother's hand assured me I was safe and back home.

"The Rabbi spoke to us briefly, instructing us to keep my resurrection secret. Yet the whole town knew I had died, and then witnessed me walking and talking among them. My body felt stronger than it ever had in my twelve years of life, free from pain and disease."

Tanya's face began to glow, and she struggled to catch her breath. Then, in perfect rhythm, she declared, "How can I possibly remain silent when, as a child, I was brought back from death to life, and even now live? I cannot any longer, for *I am Tamar, daughter of Jairus, ruler of the synagogue!*"

Tamar's gaze, like Asher's, fixed on another reality, and a swirling wind engulfed her, causing her hair to stand on end. She turned slightly and gave her full attention to the young man, now with longer hair and a beard. His eyes drew everyone's focus, simultaneously radiating peace and holy fear. As he gazed ahead, scanning the room, he locked eyes with Ray. His face and clothing glowed and pulsated as he elevated off the floor. With open hands and a welcoming gesture, he declared, "Now is the time to share your true identity!"

Ray breathed deeply, then began. "I was quite familiar with Jesus. He would often visit our home, sharing meals and conversation with us when traveling to or from Jerusalem. My sister Mary adored Him; sometimes I even felt a bit envious of the way she loved Him so deeply, more than even her own brother. He loved her, but He loved me too. Our older sister Martha always kept our home clean and prepared for Him and His companions, who could visit at any moment. She was always ready to serve.

"Most of my life, I had been in good health, able to take care of myself and my family. However, as I grew older I fell ill. It started with subtle shortness of breath, but soon progressed to swelling in my legs, ankles, and feet. At first, I thought it would pass, but it only worsened. I suspected a problem with my heart—it would beat rapidly, irregularly, and too strongly at times. The local doctor confirmed my fear: I had acquired a heart condition. As time passed, more symptoms appeared—fatigue, dizziness, and sudden loss of consciousness at times. Before anyone knew it, death was beckoning me.

"Martha and Mary had sent word to the Master that my illness had driven me to my deathbed, but He was in a distant land across the Jordan River. He did not come as he did for Tamar and Asher; my friend did not come this time. Instead, He explained, 'My work here is not yet complete.' In the interim, I passed away," Ray recounted in truth.

"When the Master proclaimed my illness would not lead to death but bring glory to God, no one understood the significance of His words. Why was He telling His chosen ones He was glad I had died? Did He truly love me as He said?" Ray had carried this memory for over two millennia, and the emotion of it overcame him.

Monica sat listening in silence as she openly wept, overcome with emotion. Elizabeth wrapped her arms around her and comforted her. "I don't understand. How is this possible?" Monica asked, in shock. "Where am I and what is happening to Ray?"

"According to my sister Martha, the Master had arrived four days after my death and burial. She saw Him from a distance and ran to meet Him, falling at His feet in tears. She couldn't understand why He hadn't come sooner. The professional mourners and wailers were also there. He picked up Martha and held her close. He wept for me, his old and dear friend. The deep sorrow of the moment had moved my Savior.

"Then the Rabbi Jesus came to my tomb, the place where I rested. A crowd of people followed Him, and in front of them all, He commanded they roll away the stone. No one was eager to do this, since I had been gone for four days and no doubt a pungent smell of death would permeate the air. But the hope of a miracle outweighed anyone's concerns. The keepers of the grave rolled away the massive stone blocking the entrance to my tomb.

"The Master lifted His eyes to pray. A bright light exploded into my burial chamber, and angels bowed their heads in reverence as a gentle breeze swept through the room. It was the most glorious and marvelous experience I had ever known, even better than being with Father Abraham during my rest.

"Then, a booming voice echoed through the room. *Lazarus, come forth!*' Instantly, I woke up on a cold slab, wrapped in linen and covered in spices. I couldn't walk normally. I recognized the voice of the Master and carefully moved toward the light shining through the entrance of the cave. The wraps covering my eyes blurred my vision, but I heard Him say, 'Loose him and let him go!' The same voice that called me out of that chamber, the same voice I'd heard many times before in my home, was the voice of my friend, Jesus of Nazareth.

"I believe I died for multiple reasons," he continued. "My sisters regularly reminded me of the miracle until their passing many years later. I can still hear their voices: 'Four days,' they would say, holding up four fingers. 'Four days we mourned for you, dear brother, until the Rabbi came!' Then right on cue Martha would point at me and say, 'and He made everything right!' Then they would giggle like little girls and dance around me." Ray's emotions rose to the surface.

"My friends teased me for the rest of their lives. They'd often ask about my 'ticker' or pretend to fall dead to the ground, then jump up 'alive'; we'd burst into joyous laughter! My miraculous experience became so well-known that people would travel for miles just to see me, to see if it was true. They would jostle me as I shopped at the market or attended synagogue, eager for a touch of the man brought back to life by the Master.

"For a couple generations, I served as a living testimony to great leaders of 'The Way,' including Justin Martyr, who sought me out for first-hand accounts of the Master's works, and my Greek friends Irenaeus and Clement, without whom none of us as Christians would be here today. These friends were contemporaries of the apostles and were taught by them to carry on the tradition and teachings of the Master. I lived as a celebrity until I eventually moved away, seeking anonymity.

"But above all, I testify to the truth of my story because I experienced death myself. I went into the bosom of Abraham, one moment alive in pain and sickness, and in an instant, transferred to a place of serenity, indescribable peace, and joy. Angels awaited and welcomed me with open arms, as if I had always belonged there. Today, I testify to each and every one of you that this is true. Heaven is real!"

A strange peace and strength filled the room, stilling everyone. In one swift motion, Ray stood tall and rigid, a bright aura emanating from his entire being as he proclaimed with conviction, "I am here because of the One who holds power over life and death, for *I am Lazarus of Bethany!*"

The swirling breeze that had enveloped Tamar swooped around Lazarus and Asher, separate from anyone else in the room. The strong current of the wind stiffened Lazarus's hair and all three elevated off the platform. Everyone watched in wonder; it violated every law of physics.

In an instant, a bright light shot out from the once young man, now fully matured, with still longer hair and a full beard, dressed in clothes whiter than snow. His entire body radiated light. He slowly raised his arms toward Asher and Tamar while gazing directly into Lazarus's eyes. A warm light emanated from his arms and eyes; he connected the three individuals to himself with it. "And I am Michael! I stand in the presence of God."

His appearance transformed to that of an angelic being over twelve feet tall. He sprouted wings, appearing from nowhere, then spread them wide, defying all natural law. "The Holy One of Israel has sent me to bring you good news and glad tidings. It is time for His faithful servants to come home."

Everyone collapsed in shock and awe at the brilliant light and holy moment, most hiding their faces, unable to look directly at the archangel as he continued speaking to the three. "As your forefather, Elijah, ascended into heaven before the throne of God by a chariot and horse of fire in a mighty whirlwind, you too shall now be taken, for the One who bound you in His glory is now calling you home. Come now and enter into His rest, and His eternal glory!"

As he finished, an ever-expanding light descended from above, piercing the center of the dome and spreading as a cloud across the entire ceiling of the temple. The onlookers in the room gasped in awe as they pointed to the miraculous event. The archangel gently flapped his wings and slowly ascended into the light, proclaiming, *"Holy, holy, holy is the Lord God*

Almighty, who was, and is, and is to come." The light fully engulfed him, causing the cloud to rotate sideways like a horizontal Ferris wheel. As if pulled by a jet stream, Lazarus, Tamar, and Asher raised their arms to heaven and rose up toward Michael and the light.

Asher reached the cloud first, his outstretched fingers creating a swirl of red mist within the depths of it. He soon disappeared, the red blending perfectly with the rotating cloud. Julie stood, gasping, hand covering her mouth as she reached in vain for her beloved.

Michael's praise continued to echo out from the cloud: *"You are worthy, our Lord and God, to receive glory and honor and power, for You created all things, and by Your will they were created and have their being."*[17]

Tamar touched the cloud next, and a new color immediately joined the swirling mix of hues, a brilliant sapphire blue adding to the mesmerizing display. The cloud seamlessly blended the three colors, creating a perfect rainbow of red, blue, and white, then gained momentum as it rotated, swirling with increased speed until it engulfed Tamar's entire body in its embrace.

As Lazarus's body lifted from the floor, it rotated as if caught in a slow tornado. Monica's hypnotic eyes watched as he turned, revealing his face, his back, then his face again. She had never seen him like this before—so youthful and at peace. If she hadn't witnessed it, she wouldn't have believed he was her husband. God gently lifted him into the cloud. Lazarus's hand released a sudden burst of golden light within the cloud, adding to the colorful ring.

---

[17] Revelation 4:11 NIV

The voice of the angel continued resonating throughout the temple. *"Come now and receive your imperishable crowns!"*

The Crown of Rejoicing: "And God shall wipe away all tears from their eyes; and there shall be no more death, neither sorrow, nor crying, neither shall there be any more pain: for the former things are passed away."[18]

The Crown of Righteousness: "Finally, there is laid up for me the crown of righteousness, which the Lord, the righteous Judge, will give to me on that Day, and not to me only but also to all who have loved His appearing."[19]

The Crown of Glory: "For I consider that the sufferings of this present time are not worthy to be compared with the glory which shall be revealed in us."[20]

The Crown of Life: "Blessed is the one who perseveres under trial because, having stood the test, that person will receive the crown of life the Lord has promised to those who love him."[21]

Some covered their ears as Michael's voice loudly boomed from the cloud on the last declaration.

The swirling mass slowly funneled its way up and through the center of the ceiling, where it had supernaturally begun.

People dashed out of the building to follow the cloud, joined by locals who had gathered around the temple. Visitors in Israel from every part of the world stood in awe, pointing at the top of the temple where the bright white

---

[18] Revelation 21:4 KJV
[19] 2 Timothy 4:8 NKJV
[20] Romans 8:18 KJV
[21] James 1:12 NIV

cloud hovered, shining and pulsating with light. A voice cried out, drawing attention to a beam of light streaking down from the heavens.

"Is it a meteor?" someone shouted. "It looks like a shooting star," another speculated.

Michael emerged from the thick cloud, and a colossal shofar materialized in his hands. His graceful wings beat rhythmically in the wind as he lingered above the cloud. With a mighty blast, he sounded the shofar, and the beam of light shifted course in response.

"It's heading right toward us!" a woman cried, pointing toward the anomaly.

With a series of precise movements, Michael reached one hand toward the beam and the other toward the swirling cloud suspended above the temple. He laid flat, then propelled himself into the beam, and further into the spinning cloud, a mixture of vibrant white, red, gold, and blue encircling the beam; all rose upward, pulled into the sky. A deep, mighty, resonant sound akin to a trumpet blasted out of the beam, and in a split second, everything vanished into the heavens, leaving a dazzling trail of vibrant colors in its wake.

Everyone who witnessed the divine miracle trembled in awe, stunned and speechless at the sheer magnitude of God's power and grandeur. Tears flowed down some faces; others fell to their knees in worship. Still others lay motionless on the ground in reverence.

EPILOGUE

Long after the divine encounter, people began to leave, while others still stood, frozen, gazing into the sky. Most remained in a daze, unable to fully comprehend it.

As Monica sat quietly on the steps outside the church, she heard someone speaking in perfect English: "Did you get that?" Turning, she saw Mark from CCJN with a camera man scurrying around, filming.

"What are you doing here, Mark?" she shouted.

Mark turned in shock, like a kid caught with a hand in the cookie jar. "Monica . . . Hi . . ." he stammered.

"You followed us here, didn't you? You and CCJN just couldn't leave things alone, could you?"

"I am a reporter, Monica; I follow the story until I get it," he answered unapologetically. Motioning to the cameraman, they turned and maneuvered through the crowd.

"I can't believe it," she said in disgust.

"I can't believe it either," Julie said, approaching Monica from the church. "You're Monica, Ray's wife?" Julie asked, her voice shaking.

"Yes, I am. And you must be Julie," replied Monica, standing, tears welling up in her eyes. They embraced without a word; nothing could be said after witnessing such an amazing yet devastating event. They shared a unique connection: Their husbands were gone forever.

They made their way back to the sanctuary together.

In the background, Rabbi Aaronson began to speak. "The Scripture says in Hebrews 9:27, 'And as it is appointed for men to die once, but after this the judgment.'[22] The prophets Enoch and Elijah were taken up just as our friends have been taken up in the clouds. Even our Lord and Savior Jesus Christ in all of His glory was taken up in the presence of many witnesses."

He then unrolled a scroll. "If the Spirit of Him who raised Jesus from the dead dwells in you, He who raised Christ from the dead will also give life to your mortal bodies."[23] The words brought a strange comfort and hope to both Julie and Monica in their shock and sorrow, and all those listening who needed to know God, who needed spiritual resurrection.

"Brothers and sisters," he continued, "if you receive Jesus, you will also receive everlasting life and like Lazurus, Asher, and Tamar, you will be captured by love, bound in His glory forever!"

Julie leaned over to Monica, whispering, "I want to fully give my life to Christ. After today, I'm in awe of Him. And I know this is the only way I will ever see Tony again. Can you help me understand how to do that?"

---

[22] NKJV
[23] Romans 8:11 ESV

"Of course!" Monica assured her. "I have a feeling when we return home we're gonna be close friends, very close. I guess we can start that right now."

"I can't thank you enough!" Julie hesitated a moment. "I'll need God more than ever for the future in front of me. For my entire life I've been infertile, but this morning, I discovered I'm pregnant . . ."

www.ingramcontent.com/pod-product-compliance
Lightning Source LLC
Chambersburg PA
CBHW051533050726
47595CB00002B/472